MUCK AND MAGIC

Stories from the Countryside

Also by Michael Morpurgo

Friend or Foe
King of the Cloud Forests
Little Foxes
Long Way Home
Mr Nobody's Eyes
My Friend Walter
The Nine Lives of Montezuma
The Sandman and the Turtles
Twist of Gold
Waiting for Anya
War Horse
The War of Jenkins' Ear
The White Horse of Zennor
Why the Whales Came
The Wreck of the Zanzibar

Banana Books for younger readers

Conker
Colly's Barn
Jo-Jo the Melon Donkey
The Marble Crusher
Snakes and Ladders

MUCK AND MAGIC

Stories from the Countryside

Edited by Michael Morpurgo

Foreword by HRH The Princess Royal

HEINEMANN • LONDON

First published in Great Britain 1995 by
William Heinemann Ltd and Mammoth,
imprints of Reed Consumer Books Ltd
Michelin House, 81 Fulham Road, London SW3 6RB and
Auckland, Melbourne, Singapore and Toronto

Contents

Foreword by H.R.H. The Princess Royal
Patron of Farms for City Children

For most people in this day and age, their first introduction to the countryside and farms is through television, books, rhymes or may be songs. But they do not portray the reality of life. You cannot turn off or put down life in the country. There is always something to be done whatever the weather or the time of day.

Some children though, thousands each year, now have the chance to leave the cities behind them for a week each year and travel down to their farm in the countryside - it could be Nethercott in Devon, Treginnis in Pembrokeshire, Wick Court in Gloucestershire - where they put on wellies and turn themselves into proper farmers.

They muck out the cows, feed the calves, pigs and hens, herd the sheep, groom the horses, muck out sheds, make hay, pick apples, dig potatoes, cackle at the geese and gobble at the turkeys. They have, many for the first time, a taste of life and work in the countryside. And they do work - up at 7.00am and out on the farm and it does not stop until the work is done.

Farms for City Children has been enabling all this to happen since 1976. The profits from the sale of this book will help more urban children to learn for themselves how it really is to be a farmer and go milking at dawn, to plant a tree, to watch the swallows return and hear the owl calling over a misty valley at dusk. At the end of a hard days work they might help a ewe to give birth, watching the lamb breathe its first breath, or they might be gathered round the fire listening to a story; perhaps a story from this book.

Anne

BLACK AND WHITE
Rachel Anderson

Illustrated by Aafke Brouwer

How Matt Didn't Care For the Dark

The school bus dropped two people off at the crossroads, then trundled away into the dusk. It was OK for Andy. He lived in one of the cottages right here. But Matt still had a way to go. Along the lane between two blank fields of sugar beet. Then down to Lower North Higgs where the trees closed in, before coming out the other side near the meadow with the stream running through it.

It hadn't been so bad back in September when there was daylight. You could dawdle along looking for blackberries. Sweet and warm in the sun. Eat yourself silly and pick a pocketful to take home.

But once the clocks changed it was all different. Out here, at the end of the lane, the dark was so very much darker than most places.

After school, other people hired videos, went window-shopping, joined judo class, watched TV. Not here, you didn't. No pavements. No shops. No street-lights. No bus service. No nothing. They'd got a telly but

9

you couldn't get any channels properly, not without white fuzz. Something to do with the dip in the land and the height of the trees behind.

'At least we're better off than where we were before,' Mum kept saying. Trying to boost her own confidence, no doubt.

The kitchen light wasn't on. She wasn't back yet. She did an afternoon shift in the turkey farm. They were supposed to be happy turkeys. The sign outside said *Contented Turkeys Make Tender Meals* with a picture of two turkeys smiling. It wasn't much of a job, gutting dead birds till half-past five.

Mum said that maybe, come spring, she'd be able to get him a bike. Save the long walk. He could leave it in Andy's shed by day, pick it up again after school.

Even a brilliant bike, Matt knew, couldn't protect you from everything.

He fetched in the evening's firewood, his shoulders stiff and teeth clenched against the menace of moving shadows. If only they had a light out in the yard like at the turkey farm. Matt reckoned he'd rather have had that than six bikes.

How Matt Found Out About the Eclipse

He set tea ready on the table. Then, before scrumpling it up to light the fire, he glanced at yesterday's paper, checking out programmes he might've watched if it was still yesterday and if they could've got decent reception. He read bits of yesterday's news.

TOTAL LUNAR ECLIPSE DUE

In the early hours of Friday the earth's shadow will fall directly across the full moon, and one of the most visually exciting of astronomical events will occur. For the duration of the eclipse, no direct sunlight will reach the moon's surface, only light bent through the earth's atmosphere, resulting in *Gegenschein* or earth-shine. The eclipse begins at 4.40 a.m. (GMT).

Matt felt terrible. Normal dark was bad enough. Now this. The light of the moon taken away and replaced by something spooky called earthshine. He decided not to mention it to Mum. She had worries enough already.

How Matt Found Out More

No one on the school bus next morning had heard about the coming eclipse. They didn't seem bothered about it either, even when Matt explained.

'It's going to cast a dark reddish glow over the sleeping world, which'll last for approximately eighty minutes.'

'Sounds weird,' said Andy. 'I think you must've been eating too many magic mushrooms.'

However, Mr Goodwood (who knew something about everything and especially about volcanoes, earthquakes and all natural phenomena) knew about eclipses.

'Well spotted, Matthew,' he said. 'Our classical eclipse is when the shadow of one heavenly body passes over another heavenly body, thus obscuring the light. Our so-called earthshine is when most of the blue light is absorbed by Earth's atmosphere, allowing only red light through.'

Andy giggled. 'D'you think Sir's been at the magic mushrooms too?'

Sir thought it was all so terribly exciting that he decided the whole class must find out as much as they could to write up in their project books.

'Provided our sky remains clear, a total lunar eclipse of this type is a most impressive sight. Well worth watching if you're in the right place. Our rural areas are ideal. Where there's no artificial light to pollute the sky.'

What Matt Decided To Do

Matt knew he couldn't go out alone, not when even scurrying to the woodshed and back stopped his heart beating. So he tried to persuade Andy to sleep over so they could keep watch together. Andy was never afraid of anything. Snarling farm dogs, pig poo, stampeding hens, dead turkey claws.

'Please,' said Matt. 'Then we can write it up together. Be only half the effort.'

'Not likely, chum,' said Andy. 'I need my beauty sleep.'

'I thought you were meant to be my friend,' Matt said.

'Yeah. But that doesn't mean I have to sit in a freezing field all night like some Inca, just to watch the moon disappearing.'

The bus stopped at the crossroads and they both jumped down.

'See ya then,' said Andy. 'Happy viewing! Let me know how it goes.'

Never could Matt admit to Andy his terror of the dark. He was going to have to face the phenomenon alone.

'You're off to bed very early, Matt,' said Mum. 'Hope you're not sickening for some beastly bug.'

'Just tired, Mum. Did PE today.'

He set his clock for three a.m. He kept his clothes on under his pyjamas to save time. It was difficult getting to sleep knowing you'd got to be awake again in a few hours. He was half hoping he'd sleep through the alarm. He didn't.

How Matt Nearly Saw Earthshine

At three minutes past three hundred hours, he was tiptoeing quietly across the kitchen to the back door. His blanket under his arm, an apple in his pocket. In a situation like this, a dog would've been a comfort. Maybe, come the spring, he'd explain to Mum that a loyal dog would be even more useful than a bike.

He lifted the latch. It was like stepping out into an old-fashioned film. The moon through the trees was as round and white as a school dinner plate. Everything was clearly visible, each twig, bush, shining blade of grass, the tiles on the roof, the logs heaped up in the woodshed, except there were no colours, only grey and black and white.

It was easy finding his way down the path, under the barred gate, along the edge of the wood and over to the meadow with the stream running through it. A white mist hovered over the water. He saw the two horses standing together in the moonlight, quite still. Not as good company as a dog, but he was glad they were there.

From here, he had a clear view of the moon in the open sky. Just a few fluffy clouds on the horizon.

How Matt Was Disturbed by the Pollution of Sounds

He wrapped the blanket round him and settled in the hedge. Kept as still as he could. That way, he felt he was less visible to whatever might be out there, watching. He tried not to listen to his heart pumping, his breathing coming and going in noisy gasps.

He kept looking at the moon.

Sir might have been right about the absence of light pollution. But there was more than enough very peculiar sound pollution. Trees sighing, branches creaking. Small dry scrabblings down in the grass. A

snort from a horse. Then the worst one of all, the short but terrible shriek of a bird somewhere in the woods. It made Matt think of all those turkeys and whether they were still happy once they were dead.

He went on staring at the moon, waiting for the edges to begin disappearing. He thought it had started. But it was as round as ever. Still too early. He wished he had a watch.

He heard the dreadful shrieking in the woods again.

Then something began happening. But not what he expected. As he watched, he could hardly hold back his disappointment. How dare the weather do this? Those little soft clouds on the horizon were gathering together and moving nearer. They'd already blanketed half the sky and extinguished the stars. Now they were creeping towards the moon.

Matt stayed where he was and hoped. Sometimes weather changed quite fast. The sky might well clear again and he'd at least get to see the end of the eclipse.

The cloud-cover thickened. Nothing could glow through that lot. It had turned into an ordinary, cloudy night.

He was angry with the weather, with the darkness, with the moon for daring to promise so much and failing to deliver. It was stupid to have come out at all. He must go back in case Mum woke and wondered where he was.

He was just about to get to his feet when the creature appeared.

16

It came out between the trees and was moving steadily towards him, a huge white shape, as broad as an arm-span and flying level with his head. Silently, stealthily, with a ghostly pale face and dark staring eyes, it was following the line of the hedge. Matt thought it was going to crash right into him but he was too astonished to move.

But no. It came flying right up to him, looked him directly in the eye, and then lurched aside and went out over the meadow. Not a turkey's ghost, not a phantom rider, but an enormous owl.

Matt was no longer afraid. It had made eye contact and identified him as a fellow-creature of the night. He watched as it dipped along the course of the stream, then back, quartering the ground. And round again and again, lurching and searching. It must be hunting. Then, away out of sight into the woods.

So very white and so much larger than he'd have expected an owl to be. And it hadn't been afraid of him.

Where did it live? What did it do all day? And why did it shriek when owls were supposed to go tu-whit, tu-whoo?

Up till now, Matt realised, fear had been obscuring his vision of everything that was out here waiting to be seen. If he'd never come out, he'd never have known.

By morning, it was raining heavily. But Matt, walking up to the crossroads, kept his anorak hood back. Then he could watch the trees. I know you're in there somewhere, he thought.

How Matt Wrote Up His Project

That afternoon, everybody else in library time was
scrabbling for the books on astronomy. Matt looked up
birds.

> Nests in old barns or big trees with suitable holes . . .
> Should be given every protection . . . Fast becoming rare
> in many areas . . . A variety of calls, the most common
> being a loud shriek . . . also makes hissing and snoring
> noises . . .

Yes, that was surely a barn owl he'd seen, going about
its night-time business, and which had looked right at
him. And that was what he wanted to write about.

After all, he hadn't, strictly speaking, seen anything of
the eclipse so how could he write about it?

He went back to his desk. He opened his project
book.

On second thoughts, maybe he'd keep the sighting of
the barn owl to himself for a bit. Though he just might
mention it to Mum.

He picked up his pen.

> *Total Lunar Eclipses,* he wrote and underlined it firmly.
> *An eclipse is any obscuring of light from one heavenly
> body by another.*

BELLA'S DEN
Berlie Doherty

Illustrated by John Lawrence

We always came down the lane on our horses. We galloped faster and faster, mud flying round us, and Polly leaping behind. We had to rein the horses in really hard when we got to the farm gate in case they tried to leap over and sent us flying. Then we tethered them to the fence. Bella's was called Cowboy and mine was called Jet. We had to leave them at the fence because they'd never make it through the next bit. They weren't really horses, you see. They were bikes.

I'd been playing horses with Bella for weeks before she told me about the next bit. She'd never told anyone else about it, and she had to get to know me pretty well before she told me. I had millions of friends where I lived before, all in my street, and all the way down town to school. But here there was only one person to play with for miles, and that was Bella. And Polly, but you couldn't count on her because she wasn't even allowed out with us at lambing time. So it was a good job I got on with Bella.

I didn't always, though. She had an annoying habit of

19

disappearing. Sometimes if we had an argument about whose horse had won or whose turn it was to close the farm gate she would just stand there with her face closing up as if she was thinking, I don't have to play with you, you know. I'd go back to shut the gate and she'd disappear. I just didn't know how she did it. Polly went too. It was no use waiting for them or shouting their names. I'd just have to wheel my horse back home and sit watching telly, like I used to do when we first came here. She had a secret, Bella had, and she was pretty good at keeping it.

Then one day she seemed to make up her mind about me. It was her turn to shut the farm gate and I said, 'Bella, I wish you'd tell me where you go when you disappear.' And she did. This is what you do.

You stand by the fence just where there's a patch that's always muddy. You can just tell where the barbed wire has been stretched. You look both ways, up and down the lane. Then you duck under the wire and slither down a really steep slope. It's no good clinging on to plants or branches because they'd just come away with you. But if you look carefully you can just make out Bella's path, a thin zigzaggy line like the tracks that sheep and rabbits make. You have to roll down the last bit, there's no other way, and you have to jump up sharp because you've come to the river then. It isn't very wide just there so it's easy to leap across it, but I advise you to wear wellies anyway.

Now you're on a little bare hill with holes in it. You

scramble up this and duck under some branches and there it is.

'There,' said Bella. 'My den.'

To tell you the truth, I was a bit disappointed at first.

The roots of a tree jut out like a shelf, and underneath them is hollow. There are strands of grass and moss trailing over it, and when you lift them up there's a bit of an old ladder, and part of a crate making a door. There's a sheep's skull nailed onto the door, with some teeth missing and half a horn broken off. You crawl in through the door and pull the grasses down. It's dark and damp and it smells of earth. It smells a million years old.

And there you are, huddled right in so nobody can see you. But you can see out. It's so quiet. All you can hear is the river, like a long, long sigh.

'I bet nobody ever comes here,' I whispered.

'Nobody knows about it,' Bella whispered back. 'Except me.'

And me now.

But that's not all.

If you scramble out and look round in the bed of mosses by the hill you can see there's a loose tufty bit that's not attached to anything. Lift it up and you've found the treasure trove. There are pieces of crockery with lovely patterns on. Some of them have gold on. And there's a brooch of Santa Claus with a bent pin.

It's still not all. There's pools around here that nobody would find even if they came searching for them.

There's Midge Pool and the Bog of Eternal Stench, Stinkweed Bog (that's where we empty out our cups of nettle tea) and Rowan Hole. Over there in the leaf bed is where the hedgehogs sleep. They'll be there till spring. And there's Minibeast House, where we put all the insects and bugs that need looking after.

And it's still not all. Underneath the bare mound there's a patch that's all peaty and black, and at one time nothing grew there at all. But do you see those trees? Twigs really, you might think, but they're growing, they really are.

'They're twice as big as they were when we put them in last year,' Bella told me.

'We?'

'Tom and Jessica.'

I can't tell you how jealous I felt then. This was our den. It belonged to me and Bella. I'd never even heard of Tom and Jessica. 'You said you hadn't told anyone else about it,' I said. I felt like pulling up those twigs.

'I found it at the same time as they did. We were together,' Bella said. 'So how could I have told them about it? We planted the trees the day they left, ages before you came. One for each of them.'

'Don't they come any more?' I was beginning to feel a bit better.

'Of course they don't. They live miles and miles away now. Nobody comes here, I told you. Except me. I come every now and again to tidy up a bit. I'm looking after it. But it's not as good, on my own.'

It was a long time before I went back to the den. Bella didn't invite me, and I didn't really feel I should go there on my own. I told myself it was a silly sort of place to play in, anyway. I missed my friends. We never needed a den where I used to live. But once Bella had shown me its real secret, its deep-down dark secret, I knew for sure that it was the most special place in the world, and that it was just as much mine as Bella's.

It was a kind of dare at first. A challenge. Bella was staying at my house for the night because her mum and dad were going to be out late. We persuaded my mum to let us sleep out in the garden in Bella's tent. There really is a little campsite out on the field behind the cottages, but that belongs to the farm. I like to watch the campers sometimes, especially at night, when their tents glow like coloured moons on the grass. We didn't have a torch or a lamp in our tent. You don't need one really, especially when the moon is as full as it was that night.

We couldn't sleep because the owls were having a conversation, one in each tree in the garden. They sounded like people with really bad colds sneezing their heads off. First one would sneeze, making you jump out of your skin, and then you'd be just about to drift off to sleep when another one would answer. They kept this up for over an hour and I was all for climbing up the trees and scaring them off. Bella squirmed out of her sleeping-bag and started pulling on her wellies.

'Where are you going?' I asked.

'The den, of course.'

'Now?'

But she was off before I had a chance to discuss it with her. You don't actually discuss things with Bella. But it took me exactly five seconds to make up my mind. If Bella could do it, then so could I.

I draped my sleeping-bag round my shoulders like a cloak, stuck my bare feet in my wellies and grabbed the packet of ginger nuts. By this time Bella was out of sight. The horses were in the garage and it would have made too much noise to get them out, so I flolopped through the farmyard after her till I'd worked my feet properly into the wellies, ran over the bridge and up the lane and searched in the moonlight for the muddy patch. I heard my sleeping-bag rip a bit on the barbed wire and reminded myself to look for any torn bits on the fence next day. It would never do for us to leave tracks behind us. Then I lost my footing and slid all the way down the bank. I'm proud to say I didn't yell out. My sleeping-bag finally fell off when I was crossing the river, and I stung myself on some nettles as I was trying to rescue it. But it was all worth it, every bit of agony was worth it, because of what happened next.

We must have been in the den for nearly an hour. There wasn't room for us both to lie down so we were sitting crouched together with Bella's sleeping-bag pulled across us both. We were both staring out into the night. It was so dark then that it didn't seem to have any depth. It was like a black curtain, just too far away to reach out and touch. Then the moon slid away from the clouds and through the trailing leaves covering the den it was suddenly as clear as day. And I think I was the first to see it. I was looking at the big mound below the den, and thinking how the moonlight made it look like a theatre with the stage lights on, and how deep and black those holes were, when I caught sight of a movement. I touched Bella's arm and she let out a little breath of, yes, she'd seen it too.

It was a fox. He seemed to grow out of the darkness of the hole, and then took shape as the moon lit him. He stood as if he had been turned to stone, and he was staring right at our den, right through the leaf strands, right at me. He was locked right in to me, reading the thoughts in my mind, and I daren't move or breathe, I daren't do anything but stare back at him, till my eyes were blurring. I thought I would pass out with holding myself so still, and my skin was ice-cold, frozen cold with fear.

Then all of a sudden he seemed to relax. He turned his head slightly, and as if it was a signal of some sort out came another, and another, four more shapes looming out of the hole, each one faster than the one before, bouncing out like infants in a school playground, tumbling red and brown and silvery white. The dog fox slunk off into the shadows. The other biggish fox, his vixen, sat just where he had been, just at the mouth of the hole, her ears pricked up and her head turning from time to time as she listened out for all kinds of sounds in

25

the hills. But the three cubs had come out to play. They cuffed each other and fell over and rolled about, jumped on each other, jumped on her, hid from each other and roly-polyed right down to the river. I could hear them breathing, and scuffling with their paws, I could hear the little puffs of sound they made when they biffed each other. It felt as if it was the middle of the world, this little patch of ground where the foxes were playing, as if nothing else that was happening anywhere was as important as this.

I've no idea what the signal was, but the vixen suddenly turned her head, sharp. The cubs scrambled up the bank and one by one slid back inside it. She waited a moment, lifted her head slightly then just melted down into the hole after them, sliding like water into it. It went dark again, as if the moon had been put out. I strained my eyes and I'm not sure whether I really saw it or not, but there seemed to be another shape, like a dark fluttering where the hole was, and a dull white glow like the tip of a tail disappearing into it.

Funny, we didn't talk about the foxes the next day, Bella and I. I think we didn't need to. But I often go to the den now. Bella doesn't live here any more. She left a long time ago. I tidy round a bit and look after the trees that are growing here for Tom and Jessica. There's a little twig for Bella too, that we planted together. The fox still comes, and he always stares at me the same way, looking right through my eyes, right inside my head, before he trusts himself to bring his family out.

I haven't told anyone else about the den. I'm only telling you now because one day, if something happens to stop me from coming here, it will need looking after. It's very special, you see.

SCARED
Anthony Horowitz

Illustrated by Tony Ross

Gary Wilson was lost. He was also hot, tired and angry. As he slogged his way through a field that looked exactly the same as the last field and exactly the same as the one ahead, he cursed the countryside, his grandmother for living in it, and above all his mother for dragging him from their comfortable London house and dumping him in the middle of it. When he got home he would make her suffer, that was for sure. But where exactly was home? How had he managed to get so lost?

He stopped for the tenth time and tried to get his bearings. If there had been a hill he would have climbed it, trying to catch sight of the pink cottage where his grandmother lived. But this was Suffolk, the flattest county in England, where country lanes could lie perfectly concealed behind even the shortest length of grass and where the horizon was always much further away than it had any right to be.

Gary was fourteen years old, tall for his age, with the permanent scowl and narrow eyes of a school bully, which, as it happened, he was. He wasn't heavily built –

if anything he was on the thin side – but he had long arms, hard fists, and he knew how to use them. Maybe that was what made him so angry now. Gary liked to be in control. He knew how to look after himself. If anyone had seen him, stumbling around an empty field in the middle of nowhere, they'd have laughed at him. And of course he'd have had to pay them back.

Nobody laughed at Gary Wilson. Not at his name, not at his place in the class (always last), not at the acne which had recently exploded across his face. The last boy who had laughed at him had been both bigger and heavier than him but Gary had still sought him out in the lunch-hour and bloodied his nose. After that nobody had challenged him. Instead, they avoided him and Gary liked that. He enjoyed hurting people, taking their lunch money or ripping pages out of their books. But most of all he liked to see them avoiding him. He liked what he saw in their eyes. He scared them – and it felt good.

About a quarter of the way across the field, Gary's foot found a pot-hole in the ground and he was sent sprawling with his hands outstretched. He managed to save himself from falling but a bolt of pain shot up his leg as his ankle twisted. He swore silently, the four-letter word that always made his mother twitch nervously in her chair. She had long since tried to talk him out of using bad language. He was as tall as her now and he knew that in her own, quiet way, she was scared of him too. Sometimes she would try to reason with him, but for her the time of telling had long since passed.

He was her only child. Her husband – Edward Wilson – had been a clerk at the local bank until one day, quite suddenly, he had fallen over dead. It was a massive heart attack, they said. He was still holding his date-stamp in one hand when they found him. Gary had never got on with his father and hadn't really missed him – particularly when he realised that he was now the man of the house. The house in question was a two-up, two-down, part of a terrace in Notting Hill Gate. There were insurance policies and the bank provided a small pension so Jane Wilson was able to keep it. Even so, she'd had to go back to work to support Gary and herself . . . no need to ask which of the two was the more expensive.

Holidays abroad were out of the question. As much as Gary whined and complained, Jane Wilson couldn't find the money. But her mother lived on a farm in Suffolk and twice a year, in the summer and at Christmas, the two of them made the two-hour train journey up from London to Pye Hall just outside the little village of Earl Soham.

It was a glorious place. A single track ran up from the road past a line of poplar trees to a Victorian farmhouse, all oak beams and gables. This was Windwhistle Farm where Jane and her sister had been brought up. Later, with the sister moving to New Zealand and Jane in London, her mother had moved into a cottage just round the corner. The track seemed to come to an end but then it twisted through a gap in a hedge and there was Pye Hall; a tiny, lopsided cottage painted a soft Suffolk pink in a sea of daisy-strewn grass.

'Isn't it beautiful?' his mother had said as the taxi from the station rattled up the lane. A couple of black crows swooped overhead and landed in a nearby field.

Gary had sniffed.

'Pye Hall,' his mother muttered. 'I was so happy here once . . .'

Where was it? Where was Pye Hall? As he crossed what he now realised was a quite enormous field Gary winced at every step. He was also beginning to feel the first stirrings of . . . something. He wasn't actually scared. He was too angry for that. But he was beginning to wonder just how much further he would have to walk. And how much further he *could* walk. He swatted at a fly that was buzzing him and went on.

Gary had allowed his mother to talk him into coming, knowing that if he complained hard enough she would be forced to bribe him with a new CD for his Discman – at the very least. Sure enough he had passed the journey from Liverpool Street to Ipswich listening to the latest release from Blur and had been in a good enough mood to give his grandmother a quick peck on the cheek when he arrived.

'You've grown so much,' the old woman had exclaimed as he slouched into a battered leather armchair beside the open fireplace in the front room. She always said that. She was so boring.

She glanced at her daughter. 'You're looking thinner, Jane. And you're tired. You've got no colour at all.'

'Mother, I'm fine.'

'No, you're not. You don't look well. But a week in the country will soon sort you out.'

A week in the country! As he limped onward and onward through the field, swatting again at the wretched fly that was still circling his head, Gary thought longingly of concrete roads, bus stops, traffic and Burger Kings. At last he reached the hedge that divided this field from the next and he grabbed at it, tearing at the leaves with his bare hands. Too late, he saw the nettles behind the leaves. Gary yowled, bringing his clenched hand to his lips. A string of white bumps rose up, scattered across the palm and the insides of his fingers.

What was so great about the country?

Oh, his grandmother went on about the peace, the fresh air, all the usual rubbish spouted by people who wouldn't even recognise a zebra crossing if they saw one. The flowers and the trees and the birds and the bees. Yuck!

'Everything is different in the country,' she would say. 'You float along with time. You don't feel time rushing past you. You can stand out here and imagine how things were before people spoiled everything with their noise and their machines. You can still feel the magic in the countryside. It's there. All around you. The power of Mother Nature, the very spirit of the earth. Alive. Waiting . . .'

Gary had listened to the old woman and sneered. She was obviously getting senile. There was no magic in the countryside, only days that seemed to drag on for ever with nothing to do. Mother Nature? That was a good one. Even if the old girl had existed – which was unlikely – she had long ago been finished off by the cities, buried under miles of concrete motorway. Driving along the M25 at 100 m.p.h. with the roof open and Blur on at full volume . . . to Gary *that* would be real magic.

After a few days spent idling round the house, Gary had allowed his grandmother to persuade him to go for a walk. The truth was that he was bored by the two women and, anyway, out in the fields he would be able to smoke a couple of the cigarettes he had bought with money stolen from his mother's handbag.

'Make sure you follow the footpaths, Gary,' his mother had said.

'And don't forget the country code,' his grandmother had added.

Gary remembered the country code all right. As he ambled away from Pye Hall he picked wild flowers and tore them to shreds, scattering them behind him. When he came to a gate he deliberately left it open, smiling to himself as he thought of the farm animals that might now wander onto the road. He drank a Coke and spun the crumpled can into the middle of a meadow full of buttercups. He half snapped the branch off an apple tree and left it dangling there. He smoked a cigarette and threw the butt, still glowing, into the long grass.

And he did stray away from the footpath. Perhaps that hadn't been such a good idea.

He was lost before he knew it. He was tramping through a field, crushing the crop underfoot when he realised that the ground was getting soft and muddy. His foot broke through the sugar beet or whatever it was and water curled over his shoe, soaking into his sock. Gary grimaced, thought for a moment and decided to go back the way he had come . . .

. . . Only the way he had come was somehow no longer there. It should have been. He had left enough landmarks after all. But suddenly the broken branch, the Coke tin and the scattered plants had vanished. Nor was there any sign of the footpath. In fact there was nothing at all that Gary recognised. It was very odd.

That had been over two hours ago.

Since then, things had gone from bad to worse. Gary had made his way through a small wood (although he was sure there hadn't been a wood anywhere near Pye Hall) and had managed to rip his shoulders and gash his leg on a briar. A moment later, even as he was inspecting the damage, he had backed into a tree which had torn his favourite jacket, a black and white striped blazer that he had shop-lifted from Notting Hill High Street.

He had managed to get out of the wood – but even that hadn't been easy. Suddenly he had found a stream in his path and the only way to cross it had been to balance on a stick that was lying in the middle. He had almost done it too but at the last minute the stick had turned, hurling him into the water. He had stood up spluttering and swearing. Ten minutes later he had decided to have another cigarette but the whole packet was sodden, unsmokeable.

And now . . .

Now he screamed as the insect, which he had assumed was a fly but which was in fact a wasp, stung him on the side of the neck. He pulled at his damp and grimy Sonic the Hedgehog T-shirt, squinting down to see the damage. Out of the very corner of his eye he could just make out the edge of a great, red swelling. He shifted his weight onto his bad foot and winced as fresh pain shuddered upwards. Where was Pye Hall? This was all his mother's fault. And his grandmother's. She was the one who'd suggested the walk. Well, she'd pay too. Perhaps she'd think twice about how lovely the countryside was when she saw her precious cottage go up in smoke.

And then he saw it. The pink walls and slanting chimneys were unmistakeable. Somehow he had found his way back. He only had one more field to cross and he'd be there. With a stifled sob, Gary set off. There was a path of sorts going round the side of the field but he wasn't having any of that. He walked straight across the middle. It had only just been sown? Too bad!

This field was even bigger than the one he had just crossed and the sun seemed to be hotter than ever. The soil was soft and his feet sank into it. His ankle was on fire and, every step he took, his legs seemed to get heavier and heavier. The wasp wouldn't leave him alone either. It was buzzing round his head, round and round, the noise drilling into his skull. But Gary was too tired to swat at it again. His arms hung lifelessly in their sockets, his fingertips brushing against the legs of his jeans. The smell of the countryside filled his nostrils, rich and deep, making him feel sick. He had walked now for ten minutes, maybe longer. But Pye Hall was no closer. It was blurred, shimmering on the edge of his vision. He wondered if he was suffering from sunburn. Surely it hadn't been as hot as this when he set out?

Every step was becoming more difficult. It was as if his feet were trying to root themselves in the ground. He looked back (whimpering as his collar rubbed the wasp-sting) and saw with relief that he was exactly halfway across the field. Something ran down his cheek and dripped off his chin – but whether it was sweat or a tear he couldn't say.

He couldn't go any further. There was a pole stuck into the ground ahead of him and Gary seized hold of it gratefully. He would have to rest for a while. The ground was too soft and damp to sit on so he would rest

standing up, holding onto the pole. Just a few minutes. Then he would cross the rest of the field.

And then . . .

And then . . .   GALWAY COUNTY LIBRARIES

When the sun began to set and there was still no sign of Gary, his grandmother called the police. The officer in charge took a description of the lost boy and that same night they began a cross-country search that would go on for the next five days. But there was no trace of him. There was talk of old mine shafts, of quicksands . . . and worse. But nothing could be proved. It was as if the countryside had taken him and swallowed him up, one policeman said.

Gary watched as the police finally left. He watched as his mother carried her suitcase out of Pye Hall and got into the taxi that would take her back to Ipswich Station and her train to London. He was glad that she had the decency to cry, mourning his loss. But he couldn't help feeling that she looked rather less tired and rather less ill than she had when she arrived.

Gary's mother did not see him. As she turned round in the taxi to wave goodbye to her mother and Pye Hall, she did notice that this time there were no crows. But then she saw why. They had been scared away by a figure that was standing in the middle of a field, leaning on a stick. For a moment she thought she recognised its torn black and white jacket and the damp and dirty

Sonic the Hedgehog T-shirt. But she was probably confused. It was best not to say anything.

The taxi accelerated past the new scarecrow and continued down past the poplar trees to the main road.

WHERE IS THE KEY TO THE UNIVERSE?
Ted Hughes

Illustrated by Michael Foreman

In the beginning, Man had the key to the universe. It was a small key. It fitted easily in the palm of his hand. Whenever he felt like it, he could unlock the earth and take out something new. A new bird, a new animal, a new plant, a new fish, and so on. But he could take out only one thing at a time.

The earth had a great many keyholes. But they were quite hard to find. Man spent most of his time poking about among stones, turning logs over, inspecting caves, peering into pools, looking for these keyholes. Whenever he found one, he slipped the key into it and turned gently. Then with a great shuddering, with a rumbling of clouds, a quaking of mountains, a trembling of forests, the earth would open. And out would come something new. It might be no bigger than a butterfly. It might be a kind of mammoth. Whatever it was, it made Man very happy.

One day, groping in a deep spring of water, with the cold up to his shoulder, and feeling under the mossy stones down there at the bottom, he found a keyhole. He fitted the key. He turned it. The earth jumped and rumbled, a dust haze rose from the desert, great cliffs collapsed like factories. And there, in front of him, staggering a little, rubbing her eyes, her hair streaming with water, was a woman – the first woman. A wife! Man was very happy about that. Straight away he showed her his hut.

That same day, when he went to the river for lilies to decorate her hair, he saw another keyhole, plain as could be, in the middle of a flat rock just awash at the river's edge. Two in one day! That was unusual. He fitted the key and turned it, not knowing what to expect. And again the earth quaked. Some great trees at the river's edge groaned and slowly toppled into the water. But right beside Man the rock split and out rushed – a crocodile. It crashed into the river like a great boat being launched, and lashed its tail and clashed its jaws. Man was amazed. He could see it was a splendid beast, even if it did look a bit too hungry. And he thought: now if that creature was very tiny, say about as big as my little finger, it would make a pretty brooch for my new wife. The crocodile writhed and spun, churning up river mud, and clashed its jaws again, like cymbals, as it cried, 'Food! Food!' Then it dived and vanished, searching for food.

Man licked his lips. The shocking arrival of that beast had made him feel weak. He went back to his wife without picking a single lily.

'What was that big splash?' she asked. And then: 'Why are you trembling?' But Man didn't answer. He was staring at something. He could not believe his eyes. Woman was sitting on a tree root, leaning her back against the trunk. And there, between her feet, under a small rootlet of the tree, was another keyhole.

Three in one day! The crocodile had given him a scare, but still he couldn't resist trying this one. He fitted the key into its slot, and gently turned.

With a crack, the tree split from top to bottom, and the two halves sprang apart. Man's wife gave a little cry and simply fell backwards into the split.

But she came bouncing straight out again as if tossed by a giant hand. And out of the crack from beneath her bounded a peculiar beast, kicking in all directions. It landed on its four feet and immediately stopped. It stood there, rigid, its head up, its neck stiff, as if it were going to explode.

Then one of its long ears slowly drooped. Slowly its head lowered. Its eyelids lowered. Perhaps it had decided not to explode. It looked as if it might be going to sleep right there in front of them.

'Oh!' cried Man's wife. 'What a pretty creature!'

'It's a donkey!' gasped Man. And straight off he saw what a useful beast this was going to be. Quickly he tied a rope round its neck and tethered it to a tree. The donkey just stood there and let him. Then Man stepped back and gazed at it, scratching his head. A woman, a crocodile, and a donkey! All in one day. It was too good to be true!

After that, he was expecting to see keyholes everywhere. And sure enough, when he went down to fill a pot of water for the new-created donkey, his foot dislodged a big pebble that rolled down and turned over at the river's edge. And there, in the pebble's belly, was a keyhole. This was something new. A keyhole in a pebble! But he couldn't help trying his key. He steadied the pebble with his left hand and turned the key gently with his right.

The bang threw him backwards, up onto dry land. His left hand was tingling. The key felt almost too hot to hold. As he blinked away the dazzle, he saw an immense beast getting to its feet, just where the pebble had been. A gigantic balloon of a beast! With a great whumping splash, it plunged into the river, much bigger than the crocodile, much heavier. Man scrambled upright. His legs wanted to run, but he clung to a branch and stared.

'A hippo!' he shouted. At least, he thought he shouted. Actually, his voice came out as a wobbly dry croak. And that was what his wife heard, a strange croaking, as he came stumbling back towards her. When she saw his face she jumped up with a little shriek, and stood there, clenching her fists against her cheeks. But all Man could do was lean on a tree panting, staring first at his wife, then at the donkey, and shaking his head as he whispered, 'What next? What next?'

It was quite a strain, turning the key in these keyholes, never knowing what was going to come bursting out. Even so, Man couldn't wait to find the next keyhole. He was feverish with excitement, all the time. He would jerk awake in the morning and his hair would almost stand on end when he saw the key. He kept it on a string round his waist. Yes, it was still there, gleaming bright, ready to open the earth yet again. And away he went, looking for keyholes among the roots and rocks, leaving his wife behind to make pots, weave carpets, cook stews, and talk to the donkey. His wife was unhappy. She wanted to go with him. 'Stay with me,' she wept. But he had all kinds of reasons for her to stay at home. And off he would go, with the key dancing at his waist. She had to make do with the donkey.

The donkey watched all this. And after Man had gone, as she sat there sobbing, he hung his head over Woman's shoulder and let his warm woolly cheek rest against her cheek. It comforted her a lot, to reach her arm up around his neck, and scratch his ears.

At last, Woman managed to persuade Man to ration himself to one keyhole-search every three days. Two days at home with her, then one off on his own hunting the keyholes. Just to make sure he stayed with her, during those two days at home, she kept the key. She hid it in a secret place. He agreed to this, to show her that he loved her. On the third day, when she packed his lunch she would fold the key into a sandwich.

45

Then came an evil day. Man went down to the river to bring up fresh water.

As he waded out through the shallows and dipped his jar, the river bulged upwards, and a great scaly arm, churning the water, swept his legs from under him. That was no arm. It was the huge tail of the crocodile. Next thing, the crocodile was moonwalking across the bed of the deep river, holding Man in its long toothy grin, like a dog carrying a stick.

The crocodile took him to its underwater cave, beneath an island out in mid-river. Here Man found he could breathe. 'Shame on you!' he cried. 'If it weren't for me, you'd still be locked up inside that rock. Let me out.'

The crocodile blinked and grinned. 'I don't want much,' he said. 'You'll do for the time being.' He began to clean his teeth and polish the scales of his belly, getting ready for the feast. But Man was thinking fast.

'I'll tell you what,' he suddenly cried. 'You can have my donkey. He's a lot bigger than I am. A lot fatter. Let me go and you can take him instead. I'll go this minute and get him for you.'

The crocodile thought for a minute or two, then said, 'No.' And went on cleaning his teeth. 'You won't come back,' he said. 'You'll trick me.'

Man sat sweating. He was greatly afraid. Then a second brainwave came. 'But the donkey's wanting to cross the river to this very island,' he cried. 'I'm in the middle of arranging his wedding.'

The crocodile stopped and gazed at Man with his

stony eyes. 'Arranging his wedding?' he asked. 'Who's he going to marry?'

'The hippo,' said Man. 'Who else? And this is the hippo's island. She lives right here, above this house of yours. You know that.' Man licked his dry lips. He was just making it all up as he went along. But the crocodile was listening. So he continued. 'And when it's all arranged, I was going to ask you to ferry the donkey across to the hippo's island. And all the wedding guests will be with him. That would be your chance.'

The crocodile blinked. 'It's true that you are a skinny thing,' he said. 'But who are the wedding guests? They might only be rats and mice.'

Man thought of the creatures he'd released from the earth with his key. 'There's water buffalo. Oryx. Zebra. Donkey calls them his relatives because they all have hooves. And they will all travel together.'

Crocodile's eyes bulged. 'If you promise to fix it, so that I carry them across, I'll let you go. But you must promise.'

He was thinking how he'd ferry all those beasts into deep water, then simply sink with them, and stack them one by one in his larder. Food for months! He'd seen the plump zebra. He'd heard of the fat oryx. And the fame of the buffalo's sweet meat had reached even him. At last he was going to taste them all.

'I promise,' said Man.

So Crocodile brought him back through the river and set him in the shallows. But as Man waded ashore the crocodile rushed and grabbed his heel. Man fell forward with a splash, and gave a yell.

'Promise,' said the crocodile.

'I swear. I promise,' cried Man. 'I swear by the key to the universe.'

'If you break your promise,' said the crocodile through his gripping teeth, 'I will devour your children to the end of the world.'

Then the crocodile let him go.

As Man sat with his wife that evening, he told her what had happened. And he told her what the crocodile had said, that if Man broke his promise Crocodile would devour his children to the end of the world.

His wife could not believe it. She stared at him in horror. 'My donkey!' she cried. 'My darling donkey! You mean you've promised him to the crocodile?' Her voice rose to a high squeak.

He nodded. He felt dreadful. He sat on the ground with his knees up, his elbows on his knees, his hands folded over the back of his neck.

'Just to save your own skin?' his wife went on, becoming more and more angry. 'You're going to let the crocodile swallow my donkey?'

Man's head sank between his knees. His voice came in a whisper. 'My skin is quite valuable,' he managed to say. 'At least, it is to me.'

His wife began to sob. 'You'll have to tell him what

you've done,' she cried. 'You'll have to tell him. Oh, my donkey! Oh! Oh!'

Man nodded again. He was thinking: perhaps the donkey will be a good fellow and let the crocodile eat him. Perhaps he will say: 'You gave me life, o master, with the key to the universe. In everything I obey you. Lead me to the crocodile. I welcome this chance to be noble, and to lay down my life, in the crocodile's dish, to save yours.'

But though he hoped the donkey would say this, he didn't think it was very likely.

So Man came to the donkey and sat down in front of him, and told him what had happened, and what he had promised the crocodile. The donkey listened, moving one ear so that it stood up straight. When Man had finished, he let the ear droop again and just went on standing there, saying nothing.

Man waited, his head bent low. After a while, he peeped up at the donkey. 'Well,' he asked, 'what shall we do?'

'You've made a mistake,' said the donkey.

Man let out a wail, flinging up his hands. 'Oh, haven't I just! What a stupid creature I am! It's all my fault.'

He wanted the donkey to feel sorry for him. But the donkey only said, 'So you'll have to pay for it.'

Man looked up, alarmed. Pay for it? What did the donkey mean? 'How?' he asked. 'How do I pay for it?'

'It's quite easy,' said the donkey.

'Then tell me, quick,' cried Man. 'How? How? How?'

'There's something the crocodile would like better than me. Better than the buffalo, the oryx and the zebra. And better than all of us together.'

'Oh, what? What?' Man jumped to his feet, suddenly full of hope.

'Something,' said the donkey.

'But what? What something?' Man was afraid that the donkey would refuse to tell him. He knew what this donkey was like.

'Promise to do it my way,' said the donkey.

'Do what?' cried Man – he could have whacked the donkey at that moment.

'My plan,' said the donkey.

Man sat down. He forced himself to be patient. He waited. He knew he would have to do it the donkey's way. 'OK,' he said. 'I promise. Let's hear it.'

Then the donkey began, speaking slowly. 'I will go to the crocodile,' he said, 'and offer him something he will not be able to refuse. I will offer him the key to the universe. So whenever he feels hungry he can find a keyhole, open the earth, and gobble up whatever jumps out. That would give him an everlasting food supply. And every meal a surprise. So go now to your wife, get from her the key to the universe, and give it to me now, and I will go.'

Man stared. He jumped up. He clenched his fists. 'Never!' he shouted. 'Nobody will ever take the key to the universe from me. Never, never, never, never, never.'

The donkey stood, lowered his head a little lower, and said nothing.

Then in a rage, Man tied a new strong rope around the donkey's neck. 'I'll show you who's master,' he cried. 'Come on, to the crocodile.' And he pulled.

The donkey dug in his feet and refused to budge. Then Man began to whack him with a stick till the stick shattered. And still the donkey refused to move.

'To the crocodile!' yelled Man. 'You ungrateful beast! Do as you're told. To the crocodile!'

Then he cut another stick, bigger than the first, and beat the donkey till that stick too shattered. But still the donkey refused to move.

Man's wife heard the shouts and came running. Man told her what the donkey had said. 'He thinks the key to the universe is just any old rusty key,' he shouted. 'He wants to give it to the crocodile. And we shall have exchanged the key to the universe for a donkey – a stubborn, impudent donkey!'

And he ran off to cut another stick, bigger than the other two. 'I'll drive him right down the throat of the crocodile,' he shouted, as he searched the thicket.

But Man's wife embraced the donkey's neck and kissed his nose. 'You are clever!' she whispered. 'You are wise! My big-eared, woolly-faced beauty! Here is the key. Go now to the crocodile. Quickly! Quickly!' And she untied the rope.

The donkey grabbed the key between his teeth and set off at a gallop. He came over the top of the river bank

in a cloud of dust. He churned down through the sand to the river's edge. Then he lifted his head and shouted, 'Crocodile! Crocodile! Take the key of the universe in exchange for the children of Man.'

The river flowed broad and strong, twirling its fringes. The reeds of the islands bowed in the wind.

The donkey roared again: 'Crocodile! Crocodile! Take the key of the universe in exchange for the children of Man.'

It was a long roar, and he roared it with all his might. It took all his breath.

He tried it again and again. He knew that any minute Man would come after him, with a bigger stick than ever. Where was the crocodile?

Donkey did not know it, but the crocodile had already arrived. It lay under the water, close to the bank, its eyes only half a centimetre beneath the surface, watching the donkey. What's he shouting about? he thought. What is this key to the universe? What do I want with a key? I want the donkey. And I see Man has cheated me. Where is the buffalo, the oryx and the zebra?

Still, a donkey was better than nothing. So the crocodile waited for the donkey to put a foot into the water. Then he would rush at him like a torpedo, knock him over, grab him and away.

But the donkey kept well up the bank.

So the crocodile stayed hidden.

And as the donkey went on shouting, his throat grew

rough and hoarse. Then suddenly, just as he had feared, Man was there, waving the big new stick.

The donkey gave a gulp, swallowed the key, and began to gallop. He galloped and galloped, but at last Man caught him and beat him and beat him.

'Stop!' cried Man's wife, but Man would not stop till that biggest stick was shattered, then he sat down. 'The key to the universe!' he wept. 'The key to the universe! Where is it? Where is it?'

His wife stroked and cuddled the donkey's head. 'Did the crocodile take it?' she asked gently. 'Did he agree to the exchange?'

Poor donkey!

He stood there, hanging his head. And Man's wife whispered in his ear, 'What did you do with the key?' And Man trembled with rage, and kept muttering, 'The key to the universe! Where is the key to the universe?'

The donkey knew where it had gone, but there was nothing he could do about it.

So that's how it happened.

That's why the crocodile lies in the shallows, waiting for the children of Man. Because, says the crocodile, Man broke his promise to me.

And that's why Man's wife is always cuddling the donkey's head, and whispering in his ear, and scratching his back.

And that's why Man is always sitting with his head in his hands muttering, 'Where is the key to the universe?'

then occasionally getting up in a wild rage and beating the donkey with a stick.

And that's why, now and again, the donkey lifts its head and roars and retches in such a terrible way that all other creatures look at him with amazement. What he's trying to say is: 'Crocodile! Crocodile! Take the key to the universe –' and all the rest of it. But he no longer has any hope that the crocodile will hear or understand him. So he shouts in hopelessness. And nobody can tell what he's trying to say any more because the key is still stuck in his throat. And he always ends up simply coughing to dislodge that key.

In vain! The key to the universe is firmly stuck in the donkey's throat.

THE RATS OF MEADOWSWEET FARM
Dick King-Smith

Illustrated by Anthony Browne

Farmer Green had grey hair and a red face. The clothes he wore were always brown, partly because they had started out brown and partly because they were covered in cow muck and pig muck, though now and again they were spotted with white, which was chicken muck.

Farmer Green only ever had a bath when there was an H in the month, though to be fair he often took several baths in March to make up for the rest of the year.

Mrs Green had been kicked on the nose by a cow when she was quite young, so, luckily, she had no sense of smell.

Farmer Green's dogs thought he smelt lovely, a mixture of sweaty body and filthy clothes and the beautiful rich smell of the dung-heap. The dung-heap was at the very heart of Meadowsweet Farm. It stood foursquare in the middle of the farmyard, looking like a huge plum-cake, and, my word, was it fruity!

Onto it Farmer Green put all the dung from the cowshed and the pigsties and the chicken-house, and every other sort of stuff that would rot down and turn into lovely rich manure. Addled eggs were flung upon it, and dead chicks too, and rotten apples, and all kinds of household waste like tea leaves and bacon rinds and fish skins and potato peelings, and, in hot weather, milk gone sour and stock gone bad. And when Mrs Green killed a chicken or Farmer Green shot a rabbit, onto the dung-heap went feathers and skins and guts.

From its base dark brown liquids oozed, and from its top rose little wisps of steam as the great cake cooked.

There were certain animals, of all the different kinds on the farm, that thought the dung-heap was an earthly paradise.

These were the rats. Meadowsweet Farm was running with rats.

As well as being dirty, Farmer Green was a wasteful careless man, who would always rather not bother than take trouble. He did not store corn or pigmeal or cowcake in metal bins, but left them in sacks, which were no protection against sharp teeth. So that the rats always had masses of food to eat, as well as all the lovely rotten titbits they found on the dung-heap.

The rats of Meadowsweet Farm were of all sizes, from babies to big old bucks, but whatever their ages, all had one thing in common. They were fat.

They were also much too clever for Farmer Green. He put down poison for them, but they never touched it. He set traps for them, but they never sprung them. Things might have been different had there been cats around, as there are on almost every farm. But Farmer Green didn't like cats.

'Can't stand 'em,' he would say. 'Too clean by half. Forever washing theirselves, they are. 'Tisn't natural.'

Thus, over the many years that Farmer Green had been at Meadowsweet Farm, the rats multiplied, and grew, not only fatter, but bigger and stronger in each generation. Big bucks and does produced larger and larger children, who in their turn grew up to have children bigger yet.

But one rat was by far the biggest of all.

As sometimes happens when a great many rats are gathered together, there appears one day a creature (always a male) so huge that he dwarfs all the other members of the colony.

He is ratlike in every way except that he is the size of a small dog, and he rules the colony unchallenged, taking his pick of the does as mates, and indeed dealing out death to any rat that offends him.

This monster is known as the king rat, and there was such a one at Meadowsweet Farm, and his name was Ripper.

Farmer Green had never set eyes on the king rat. Ripper was far too cunning. He knew what the farmer's gun did to rabbits, and he had no wish to finish up on the dung-heap. So he kept to his den by day, only emerging after dark.

Ripper was much too big to get down an ordinary rat-hole, but he had found a perfect hiding-place. The chicken house backed onto a wall, and between house and wall there was a narrow weed-filled space. Among these weeds, a fox had dug a hole, tunnelling right under the chicken-house. One night, he must have reasoned, Mrs Green might forget to shut up her fowls, and then he would be nice and handy. What he had not expected was to return from hunting early one morning to find his earth occupied.

From the entrance came a strong smell of rat, and the fox hastened down the tunnel, eager to kill the intruder and breakfast off rat meat, only to get the shock of his life.

Suddenly he was confronted by a monstrous creature almost as big as himself, that showed all its very large teeth and chattered at him in fury. The fox fled.

By daytime, then, Ripper kept to his den, rat-napping in between visits from his troops. The king rat had organised the rats of Meadowsweet Farm into a private army, enlisting the most intelligent among the younger animals as his personal bodyguard.

Not that his great body needed guarding – he was quite capable of looking after himself – but these picked followers all had particular duties.

Some acted as lookouts, keeping watch on Farmer Green and his wife and the dogs all through the daylight hours.

Some acted as reporters, bringing news of everything

that happened on the farm – a lorry delivering a load of corn or meal, the latest positions of traps or poison baits, the most recent titbits on the dung-heap.

And some attended upon the king rat as servants, bringing tasty morsels of food for him, which they carried in their mouths.

One morning a young buck made its way down the tunnel and squeaked for permission to enter the royal den.

'Come in!' growled Ripper, and, 'What is it?'

'Please, sir,' said the young buck (very respectfully, for to offend the king in any way, however slight, was to commit suicide), 'there's a dead hen in the chicken-house above.'

'Fell off its perch, eh?' said Ripper. 'Thought I heard a bump in the night. Right then, wait till they throw the bird onto the dung-heap, and then,' he licked his lips, 'see that the heart and the liver are brought to me, understand?'

'Yes, sir,' said the young buck. It was about to turn and go when, luckily, it remembered the correct way to leave the royal presence and backed out of the den.

When Mrs Green came to let out the flock, she saw the dead hen on the floor of the chicken-house, and picked it up by its cold yellow legs. She carried it down the yard and flung it on top of the dung-heap.

Farmer Green caught sight of her doing this as he finished milking his cows (whose udders he never washed) with his filthy dirty hands, and an idea suddenly struck him.

He went into the farmhouse and fetched his gun. Then he entered the stables and climbed a flight of steps to a loft above, a loft whose window gave a perfect view of the yard below and the dung-heap in its centre and the dead hen in the middle of the dung-heap.

Farmer Green loaded both barrels, sat down upon an old box, and waited.

For a while nothing happened. The morning sun rose higher in the sky, the only sounds to be heard were occasional cluckings or gruntings or the low of a cow, while sparrows chirped on the stable roof. The smell of the dung-heap filled the air.

Then suddenly, silently, rats began to emerge from buildings all around the yard. Some knew of the king's orders, some had only heard that there was a dead hen to be had, some knew nothing but were merely following their fellows.

Up onto the dung-heap climbed a host of brown scaly-tailed shapes, heads raised as they sniffed, whiskers twitching. Then, with a rush, they flung themselves upon the carcase of the hen.

There was a chorus of squeaks and squeals as, in a cloud of feathers, they tore at the body, despite the cries from those who knew of: 'Not the heart or the liver! Keep the heart and the liver for the king!'

Farmer Green waited until the excitement was at its peak, till a scrum of rats was fighting over the hen in a solid mass. Then he poked out his gun from the window of the loft above and fired both barrels into the mob.

Lying in his den, waiting for his breakfast to be served, Ripper heard the double crash of the gun, and then, after a while, a nervous squeak in the tunnel, asking permission to come in. When it was given, he saw, not the original messenger, but a scared young doe.

'Well?' said Ripper. 'What was the man shooting at? Rabbits?'

'No, sir,' said the doe.

'What then?' said Ripper. 'And where's my breakfast? The heart and liver from that hen, that's what I ordered. Where are they? Where's that young fellow I gave the orders to? I suppose he's gone and let the rest of them eat the lot? I'll kill him, see if I don't!'

'Please, sir,' said the young doe, 'he's already dead. Along with a great crowd of them. On the dung-heap. The man shot them all. There are thirty rats dead there, they say, sir, please, sir, sorry, sir.'

For a while there was an awful silence in the depths of the fox-earth. Ripper crouched in the gloom, staring, it seemed to the young doe, right through her. In fact he was not seeing her at all, did not notice as she cautiously backed away.

All he saw, in his mind's eye, was a ghastly pile of bodies on top of the dung-heap. Thirty bodies, no less, thirty, he did not doubt, of the bravest and the best.

'He will pay!' snarled Ripper through his teeth. 'That man, he will pay for this!'

By nightfall the numbers of rats had fallen by more than thirty. Another dozen had hurriedly left the farm to find some other place to live. These were the lookouts who had failed in their duties. They should have seen the farmer go in and fetch his gun, and have reported it to the king. But they hadn't, and the penalty for such a failure was, they knew, death.

At dusk, Ripper came out of his den in a fury. He sent messengers with orders that every rat was to come to the barn at moonrise.

In silence they waited, rank upon rank of them ranged across the floor, every eye upon the king rat, who crouched above them on a pile of straw bales, motionless, menacing.

At last he spoke.

'Rats of Meadowsweet Farm,' said Ripper, in a voice so harsh that the white owl perched among the roof timbers, looking hungrily down at the assembled company, flew hastily out through the owl-hole.

'Tonight we are gathered together,' went on the king, 'to mourn the loss of thirty brave comrades. Those who caused their deaths by their inattention to duty would also be dead by now had they not fled like the cowards they are.'

Here Ripper paused, and looked at each rat in turn, and each rat in turn felt a cold thrill of fear.

Then the king rat spoke again.

'If there are cowards left among you,' he said softly, 'come forward.'

No one moved.

'Good,' said Ripper. 'For you will need all your courage. Tonight we seek revenge upon the man who murdered your mates. Listen carefully, each and every one of you.'

Ripper's plan was an ambitious one, no less than the invasion of the farmhouse itself. He aimed to do maximum damage, first to the place, and then to the man himself.

Because Farmer Green was so lazy and slipshod, the house at Meadowsweet Farm was practically falling down, and there were holes and gaps and broken panes everywhere, through which rats could enter. Ripper's orders to the bulk of his troops were simply to get inside the house (the dogs were chained to their kennels in the yard) and do the greatest possible damage.

'Eat any food you can find,' he said, 'and what you cannot eat, befoul. Foul the carpets also, and chew holes in the furnishings, and spoil and destroy wherever you go. And if you find electric wires, bite through them.' (Which will kill you, I'm afraid, thought Ripper. But like any general, he knew that soldiers must die in battle.)

Then he called for volunteers.

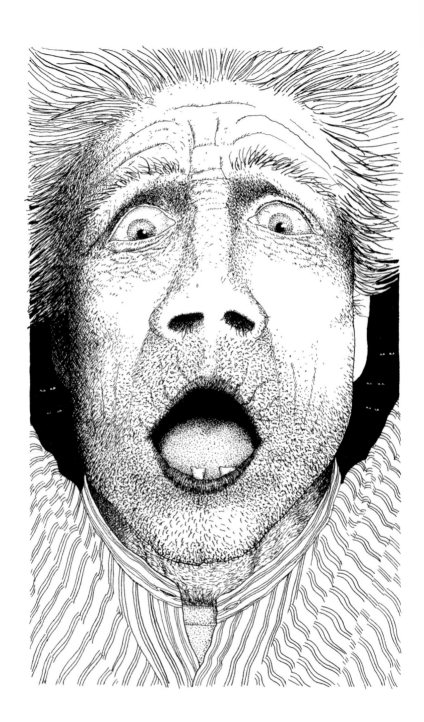

'I want good climbers,' he said, and a chorus of voices cried, 'Me, sir! Me, sir! Me!'

Ripper picked ten from these.

'Your job,' he said to them, 'will be to scale the wall of the house – there is creeper on it, to make things easier – and get in through the open window of the room where the man and woman sleep.'

'Shall we attack them, sir?' asked one eagerly.

'No. Hide beneath the bed, all of you, and keep still and quiet. Then in the early morning when the man gets out of bed to go and milk his cows, wait till he is at the top of the stairs. Then rush at him, squeak and squeal and bite at his ankles, and with any luck he will lose his balance and fall down the stairs. And if, as I suspect, they are steep, and because he is heavy and clumsy, he will, I sincerely hope, break his neck.'

Ripper waited until the small hours before he sent in the first of his troops. They had orders to avoid disturbing the dogs, and to do their work of destruction as silently as possible, and they did it well.

Just before dawn, Ripper sent up the climbing patrol. By the time Farmer Green's old tin alarm clock went off, the ten were under the bed, waiting.

It was still dark, so the farmer pressed the light switch, but nothing happened. (Downstairs lay the singed body of the rat who had bitten through the mains supply.)

'Electric's off,' he said to his wife, 'and there's a terrible smell of rat in here.'

'I can't smell anything,' said Mrs Green sleepily.

Farmer Green dressed (which consisted of pulling on his trousers, for he always slept in shirt, socks and underwear) and went out of the bedroom in his stockinged feet.

Ten rats followed silently.

As he reached the head of the stairs, feeling his way in the darkness, they charged.

Mrs Green heard a chorus of squeals and a loud curse from her husband, and then a thumping bumping noise as of a heavy body tumbling down the stairs.

Then there was silence.

Mrs Green never forgot that dreadful day.

First, there was the finding of her husband unconscious upon the floor at the foot of the stairs. Then, once she had dialled 999 and was waiting for the ambulance, there was the discovery of all the damage done in the kitchen and the other downstairs rooms of the farmhouse.

There were holes in the chair covers and rents in the curtains, little ornaments that had stood upon the mantelpiece lay smashed on the floor, books had been tipped from their shelves and their pages shredded, and there was rat muck everywhere.

As for the food in the larder, cheeses had been nibbled, eggs broken and sucked dry, and what was left of a big pan of cream was speckled with rat droppings.

Once the ambulance had left, Mrs Green went to milk the cows. This done, she set herself to tidy up. At the hospital, once they had established (holding their noses the while) that Farmer Green was suffering from concussion but had no bones broken, they first of all sprayed his recumbent form with Spring Violets air freshener. Then, once he had regained consciousness, they stripped off all his clothes and burned them, and then they saw to it that (although it was July) he gave himself a very thorough washing all over in a bath, and they changed the water several times.

Later that day, satisfied with his condition, they sent him home to Meadowsweet Farm, dressed in clean borrowed hospital pyjamas and smelling (though Mrs Green could not know this) like a big, pink, newly washed baby.

Husband and wife sat at the kitchen table, drinking tea.

Mrs Green looked at her husband's face, at his neck, his hands, his fingernails. 'You look different,' she said.

Farmer Green ran his fingers thoughtfully through his clean hair, feeling the bump where his head had struck the floor. His injury, it seemed, had changed him for the better.

'I feels different,' he said. 'Reckon I'll have a bath a bit more often. 'Tis nice.'

'It was rats,' said Mrs Green.

'Was it?' said her husband. He seemed to have forgotten the whole incident.

'You'll have to shoot some more,' said Mrs Green. 'They made a mess.'

'Not now,' said Farmer Green. 'I do feel a bit tired.'

'Well, go to bed then.'

'All right. But you go up first, and mind and put nice clean sheets and blankets on the bed. I don't want to get meself dirty.'

Once her husband was in bed, Mrs Green went out to shut up her fowls as the light faded. Suddenly she saw a large brown shape come out from behind the chicken-house and glide away along the bottom of the wall. Ripper was on his way to congratulate his victorious troops.

Mrs Green shut up the chickens, returned to the farmhouse, fetched her husband's gun, loaded it, and came quietly back.

'It looked like a rat', she said to herself, 'but no rat was ever so big as that. Maybe t'was a badger. Anyways, I'll bet he was after my hens.'

And she waited.

In a little while the moon rose, and not long after Mrs Green saw the large brown shape slinking back along beneath the wall. She waited until the creature was within point-blank range, and then she pressed both triggers.

The recoil was such that she fell over backwards.

As for Ripper, the king rat, he fell dead.

It was a weary Mrs Green who dragged herself up to bed that night, her shoulder bruised by the discharge of the gun, her back and arms aching from the effort of lugging the body of her victim to the dung-heap.

Somehow she had managed to heave it up on top, where it lay among the bodies of those her husband had shot, its great teeth bared in a grin of death.

She climbed into bed beside her husband (who smelled so sweet though she was unaware of it) and said, 'I shot ever such a big rat.'

'Oh ah?' said Farmer Green sleepily.

'We'll have to get rid of them, you know.'

'Of what?'

'Rats.'

'Oh ah.'

But the strange thing is that the Greens had no need to do this. It must have been the sight of the dead body of their king, because when the sun rose on the following morning, there was not a single one left (nor did one ever return) out of all the rats of Meadowsweet Farm.

MR HASBINI'S GARDEN
Elizabeth Laird

Illustrated by John Vernon Lord

The boy was in the hospital office when the fighting started.

'Who are you looking for? What was his name again?' The clerk began to leaf without interest through a stack of files.

'Ramzi, I told you,' the boy said. 'He was at the secondary school. The one that was bombed. He's sixteen.'

'Didn't you come in here a few weeks ago?' the clerk said, looking up with a frown of irritation. 'I told you then that we'd had no boy of that name here.'

'But he might have been brought in later,' the boy said. 'Please. Please look.'

With no warning and with deafening force, a shell exploded near by. The clerk disappeared under his desk as fast as a mouse bolting into a hole.

The boy darted to the door and out of the building. He began to run, terrified of being inside in case the building collapsed around him.

The street was empty. Bicycles lay where people had thrown them down as they had dashed for cover. But the boy preferred to take the risk of being caught in the battle to the terror of being inside. He ran low to the ground, as fast as a hare, ducking and diving to make himself a harder target.

Shouts and explosions ahead made him swerve down a side alley. He ran fast, on and on, making for the edge of town.

At last he saw ahead the open road running through sun-baked fields and groves of orange trees. His pace slackened.

'Safe,' he thought, the word pounding in his head like the blood pounding through his heart. 'Safe, safe, safe here.'

Then, on the road ahead, he became aware of a low, steady roar. The boy screwed his eyes up against the blinding sun. He could make out a group of tiny specks in the distance, growing infinitely slowly but with awful steadiness as they approached. The pulse-beat in his head changed.

'Tanks,' it went, 'tanks, tanks, tanks.'

He looked round for a place to hide, and saw, a little way back from the road, a familiar pair of corrugated-iron gates opening into a walled compound. Through them he caught a glimpse of flower-pots laid out in rows under the shade of some ancient olive trees and he ran towards them.

Mr Hasbini, ignoring the familiar rumble and stutter of fighting two miles away in the town, had been squatting on the hot hard ground in the middle of his

nursery garden slicing geranium stems and sticking them into pots full of freshly watered soil. He stood up, grumbling as his knees creaked, then pushed back his broken straw hat and scratched his bald head as he surveyed his long rows of pots.

'I'm a silly old fool,' he remarked to his pigeons, who were dozing through the midday heat in their cages under the shade of an old fig tree. 'Why do I bother? Who wants pot plants when there's a war on?'

He raised his head as he heard a distant rumble and frowned.

'Still miles away,' he said, 'but coming this way. I'd better close up in case.'

He was about to go and shut the gates when the boy ran through them into the compound. Mr Hasbini picked up a spade and shook it at him.

'Get out of here!' he shouted.

'It's all right,' panted the boy. 'It's me, Sami. You know me, Mr Hasbini. I used to come here with my dad to buy plants . . . '

'Sami? Mr Faris's son?' Mr Hasbini looked at the boy in astonishment.

'We've got to get out of here,' the boy said, dancing with impatience. 'There are tanks coming up the road. We'll be trapped!'

'And where do you suggest we go?' Mr Hasbini had rested his spade on the ground and was leaning on it. 'Up the road, into the battle in the middle of town? Or down the road towards the tanks?'

'Across the fields, through the orchards . . . '

'Don't be daft, boy. They're mined. No, we're going to stay here. Safest place to be. The tanks won't bother us. They're making for those hotheads up in town. Stop jumping up and down. You're giving me a headache. Tell me what on earth you're doing here on your own. Where are your parents?'

The boy shook back his tousled black hair and hitched up his trousers, which had grown too loose on his scrawny waist and fell in folds over his torn trainers.

'They went to my grandma's village, but I ran away. I've been on my own for weeks. I can't go till I've found Ramzi.'

'Your older brother? How did you come to lose him?'

'We were at school when it was bombed. The whole building collapsed. I got out all right, but Ramzi . . . He *must* have escaped! I *know* he did! But no one will believe me. Everyone just says . . . '

'Checked the hospitals, did you?' said Mr Hasbini.

'Yes. He's not in any of them.'

'In that case . . . ' Mr Hasbini began.

'I know what you're thinking,' interrupted Sami, his newly broken voice suddenly high-pitched with anger, 'but it's not true! Plenty of boys got out. I saw them. There was shooting everywhere just after the bomb, and I ran away. I hid for hours till the fighting stopped, and when I went back I couldn't find Ramzi. I went home, and Dad said we had to go to the village, but I wouldn't go. I've been hunting and hunting . . . '

His voice shook and he wiped his forearm across his dirt-smeared face. Mr Hasbini stopped looking at him and squatted down among his flowerpots.

'What are you doing?' said Sami after a while.

Mr Hasbini dusted earth off his hands and sliced through another geranium stem.

'Taking geranium cuttings, of course. Didn't they teach you anything at school? These bits of stalk will grow into new plants. They'll be a picture next year.'

'Huh! Next year!' The boy squatted down beside him. 'We'll all be bombed to bits next year.'

'You probably will be if you keep on running round town in the middle of a civil war,' remarked Mr Hasbini. 'But these cuttings will still grow. It won't make any difference if we're dead or not. They'll just put out roots and leaves and turn into brand-new plants.'

'So what?' Sami picked up a geranium leaf and crushed it between his fingers.

'Stop that! Where's your respect for nature?'

'I don't care about nature. Nature's a waste of time.'

'A waste of time?' Mr Hasbini cast his eyes up to heaven. 'Do you know which side's going to win this war?'

'Our side is. My dad says . . .'

'Rubbish. Nobody's going to win. Have you seen that supermarket that was bombed last year? There are trees growing right through the tarmac in the car park, and grass and flowers sprouting all over the ruins. Nature's going to win this war, that's what. Nature always wins.'

'Listen. The tanks are coming,' said Sami, lifting his head.

'Never mind the tanks. They don't mind us,' said Mr Hasbini. Carefully, he pushed another geranium stem into the waiting earth.

Sami picked up the knife.

'Can I do one?' he said.

'Yes, but take care. Don't bruise it. Look, I'll show you . . . '

They both jumped suddenly as a burst of automatic rifle fire, coming from the direction of the town but quite close by, ripped through the air. Mr Hasbini struggled quickly to his feet.

'That was close! Quick, help me shut the gates!'

Sami was at the gates in an instant, clanging the first one shut. Mr Hasbini ran after him, his stiff legs working as fast as they could. The tanks had nearly arrived outside the nursery garden, their huge caterpillar wheels clanking over the tarmac, but they stopped at the sound of gunfire, and their still-deafening engines were idling.

'Would you believe it! Those madmen are attacking the tanks!' panted Mr Hasbini as he shut the second gate and plunged the bolts home.

For a moment, they both relaxed. The nursery garden looked so peaceful, enclosed in its high wall. Except for the pigeons, who were fluttering with fright in their cages, it was almost impossible to believe that a battle was about to break out just outside.

But the ambush was only a few hundred metres away. Sami could even hear the men's voices as they broke cover; frantic questions and hoarse shouts of command.

'Can't stay here,' said Mr Hasbini. 'Gate's too flimsy. Bullets'll rip right through it,' and he began to run again, gasping for breath, towards the small concrete shed in the middle of the garden.

Automatically, Sami followed him. Then he saw where Mr Hasbini was going.

Not inside, he thought. Not trapped inside!

He looked round desperately. His instinct was to run, but there was nowhere safe to go. The pigeons were flapping their wings and pecking violently at the wire of their cages. Sami ran to them.

'Sami! Come here! What are you doing?' Mr Hasbini shouted, but Sami did not listen. He was fumbling with the latches of the cages.

'Get out! Fly away!' he shouted as he wrenched the doors open. 'You'll be trapped, you stupid birds! Get out!'

The pigeons, more terrified than ever, fluttered away from him into the backs of their cages.

'Sami! Over here!' called Mr Hasbini. Sami looked round. Mr Hasbini was not inside the shed but behind it, crouching against its concrete wall.

The noise of the battle was deafening now. Sami could not see the men running down the road directly outside the compound, but he could hear the clatter of their feet and the sharp cracks of their rifles as they let off rounds of automatic fire. He felt the dreadful trembling weakness of terror engulf him as he dropped down beside the old man.

'I'd rather be outside at a time like this,' said Mr Hasbini. 'If I'm going to die, I'd rather do it with the sky above me, looking at my garden.'

Sami nodded. In spite of the heat, he was shivering.

'I was in the science lab when the roof fell in,' he said. 'I was near the window. I only just got out. I couldn't find Ramzi. He was in the library. I was . . . ' He stopped, his lips trembling, then went on again. 'I've been hunting for three weeks, going round the hospitals, going to his friends' places, looking everywhere he might have run to if he was really scared.'

Mr Hasbini grunted. 'Why are you so sure he's still alive?'

'He's got to be! How can I be alive, and not Ramzi?'

With a deafening bang, a mortar hit the ground on the far side of the shed and exploded, splintering flower-pots and throwing earth and cuttings in all directions. Sami flinched, and covered his head with his arms.

There was a moment of eerie silence, as if the whole world was waiting. And then the tank opened fire. The 120mm shell flew over the compound wall with a deafening roar, screamed across the garden and ploughed through the wall on the far side with a bang that seemed to make the very air shake, and set the echoes flying.

Sami and Mr Hasbini had shrunk into themselves. They were squatting against the concrete wall of the shed with their arms tightly wrapped round their knees, making themselves as small as possible. Sami rocked backwards and forwards, and in the silence that followed the explosion, Mr Hasbini heard him whimpering. Not knowing what to say or how to comfort him, he began awkwardly to pat his shoulder, tears running down his own weather-beaten cheeks.

'Ramzi's dead, isn't he?' Sami said at last. 'You think he's dead.'

'Yes,' said Mr Hasbini.

Sami looked at him as if he was seeing him for the first time.

'We'll all be dead soon. What does it matter?' he cried suddenly, jumping to his feet. 'Why bother to take cover? What's the point? Kill me too, go on, get me too!' and before Mr Hasbini could stop him, he had run out from the shelter of the concrete wall and was standing unprotected in the open garden.

'Go on! Shoot me!' he shrieked at the sky, and he flung out his arms, put his head back and shut his eyes.

Nothing happened. Quietness had suddenly fallen. The battle outside was over. The only sound was the rumbling of the tanks' great caterpillar wheels as they started rolling on again up the road towards the town.

Sami opened his eyes.

'I'm alive!' he said aloud. 'Ramzi's dead, and I'm alive.'

He felt very tired and a little dizzy. He sat down on the ground.

'You certainly won't be alive much longer if you go on doing that kind of thing,' said Mr Hasbini disapprovingly as he came out from behind the shed. 'Scared me more than the tanks.'

He looked round his garden. The shell had blown a big hole in one wall and torn a branch off a tree, but most of the flower pots still stood in their neat rows, and the pigeons, who had taken off and flown around in a high circle while the battle raged, had come back to peck and strut round the grain bowls in their cages.

'See what I mean?' said Mr Hasbini with a rare smile. 'Nature always wins.'

'I want to go home, to Mum and Dad,' said Sami suddenly, rising shakily to his feet.

'That's not a bad idea,' said Mr Hasbini. 'As a matter of fact, I think I'll come with you. I could do with a few days of peace and quiet. We'll wait till it's dark. It'll be safer then. In the meantime, let's eat. I've got some food in my shed. I expect you're hungry. Boys usually are.'

Sami nodded. Suddenly he was ravenous.

'I'll only stay away for a day or two, mind,' went on Mr Hasbini. 'I'll have to get back to mend that hole in the wall and do my watering, if the water's still turned on, and feed the birds.'

'I'll come with you,' said Sami. 'I'll help you.'
'Maybe,' said Mr Hasbini. He turned towards his shed. 'Come back in the spring, anyway. You won't believe

your eyes. Those little bits of stalk will be great big geranium plants, all scarlet and orange and pink, and the cuts that made them will be quite forgotten. The world will be like a new place then. You'll see.'

THE SECRET STONES
Joanna Lumley

Illustrated by Christian Birmingham

'Look!' said Jan, wiping a squeaky space with her gloved hand on the steamy window. 'I don't remember that island being there before.' Pen leaned over and pressed her face against the glass. The school bus bumped and joggled and their breath made the window mist up again.

'Where? What island?' Pen screwed up her eyes and tried to see in the gathering darkness. The bus went round a corner and behind some trees, which gave them time to run to the back of the bus. All the children had been dropped off by now; Pen and Jan were the only ones left, except for Jacko, Pen's little brother, who was singing to himself in the seat behind the driver. The girls knelt on the back seat and peered out.

Outside, in the October evening, ground mists lay like veils in the fields. The moon was up but the only place you could see its light was on the water of the big lake. At the far side they could see the lights of their village twinkling and there, in the middle of the lake, was the island. It wasn't very big, in fact it was just a dark shape with a tree sticking out of it; but it was definitely an island and it quite definitely hadn't been there yesterday. The two girls watched it until the bus started to climb up through the wooded hills and the lake was lost from view. They sat back and looked at each other.

'Crikey!' said Pen.

'Blimey O'Riley!' said Jan.

'Let's go and see it tomorrow.'

'Only us,' said Jan.

'Absolutely only us,' said Pen, 'and no telling the grown-ups.'

'Or Jacko,' said Jan. The bus stopped with a screech at Jan's gate and she jumped off and disappeared at once.

'It's just me and Jack, Mr Phillips,' shouted Pen at the driver.

'Righto, captain,' he shouted back and Pen went to sit beside Jacko who grinned and rattled the tin of stones he always carried with him. One of his front teeth had come out already although he was only five and a half. Pen's teeth were huge but her mum had said that at nine you couldn't expect to be the right size for your teeth. Jacko didn't have to do homework as he was only in the babies' class but Pen's satchel was bulging with books that she'd have to read during the weekend.

'End of the line! Everything's fine! Goodnight, soldiers!' yelled Mr Phillips, and with a sigh and hiss the doors opened and the two children ran down the steps and into the dark lane which led to their house. As the bus drove off into the night they could hear night sounds: an owl, a dog barking, something rustling in the hedge, a sheep coughing like an old man and always the slappy-lapping sound of the lake across the water meadow.

Pen and Jacko half ran, half skipped along with Jacko holding the torch as it was his turn. Pen was only thinking of the adventure tomorrow. Jacko was burbling away in his pretend language that he used when he thought no one was listening. They could smell the woodsmoke of a bonfire, then they saw the lovely golden lights of the house and the front porch and in no time they'd kicked off their muddy shoes and rushed inside in their socks where the smell of supper made them forget everything else.

At breakfast the next morning Pen said, 'I'm going to do all my homework this morning. If I finish it, can I go out and play with Jan? And please, Dad, if we're careful can we borrow the boat? Oh please, Dad, please, dear, friendly, kind Dad . . . ' and she went round to his chair and pulled her eyes sideways and did a silly smile that always worked.

As usual Dad laughed, and said, 'Penelope Jackson, you're bats in the belfry. Thousands would say no but I'll say yes for a great big hug.' Pen put her arms round his neck and almost strangled him, she hugged so hard.

'Dad,' she said, putting on her extremely serious face which always worked, 'we don't think we should take

Jacko with us as we're not really responsible enough and we think he'd be safer not coming.' She made her forehead go into an anxious frown and blinked quickly to show how hard she had been thinking over this problem.

'Very wise, Pen,' said Mum, 'and I shouldn't think Jacko will mind much.' They all looked at Jacko who began shrugging his shoulders and making chimp noises. 'Jacko can muck around here, can't you, chimpy boy?'

Jacko went, 'Hoo, hoo,' and slithered under the table, crawled past Dad's feet and hopped out of the room.

Pen worked very hard at her homework. She had to learn two verses of a poem called 'Meg Merrilees,' do one page of sums that weren't at all hard, read one chapter of history about King Richard the Lionheart and draw a map of Australia. Just as she finished, the clock struck twelve and the telephone rang at the same time.

'It's Jan for you, Pen,' said Mum and went back into the kitchen.

'I can still see it,' whispered Jan in a hoarse voice. 'The island's still there. I'll bike over after lunch.'

'Wizard wheeze,' said Pen. 'We've got the boat.'

'Totally great!' said Jan and rang off.

Lunch was stew and baked apples. Jacko was ticked off for trying to put bits of carrots in the tin where he kept his stones. 'I want that colour,' he said in his whiny voice. 'Only that colour.' Then there was a ring at the doorbell and there was Jan, very red in the face, in her gumboots and her favourite knitted hat pulled down to her eyebrows.

She and Pen ran down the lane past the tall trees where the rooks nested, through the blackberry patch, over the stile, across the water meadow and down to the water's edge.

It wasn't really a lake, but a huge inlet from the sea. It was joined to the sea by a river at the far side, but it felt like a lake, except for the tide which rose and fell, leaving the stones glistening and patches of mud and sand shining in the thin sunlight. Dad's boat was tied up to the short wooden jetty; it looked like half a walnut shell. When they got there they couldn't speak for a few minutes, they were puffing and panting so hard.

'Look!' said Jan.

In the middle of the lake was the island. From the shore it was very hard to tell how big it was, but it certainly had a tree on it and bushes growing close to the ground. Pen and Jan untied the boat, put the oars in the rowlocks and taking an oar each they set off with a splash and a clonk. As you know, when you row a boat you have your back towards the way you're going, so they took it in turns to look round and shout directions at each other. The island came nearer and nearer until at last the bottom of the boat crunched onto the shingle and Pen jumped out to pull it ashore. The cold water went right over her boots and up to her knees but she didn't notice, she was so excited. Together they pulled the boat right up onto the narrow beach. Then there was silence.

'Oh, crikey baloney!' said Jan. 'There's smoke from a chimney.' They rustled up through the bushes towards the trees and this is what they saw. A small fire was burning and above it, on a tripod made of sticks, hung a black can with steam coming out of it. All around the clearing were bits of old carpet and there were rags spread out to dry on the bushes. There was a low bench made from driftwood and on it sat an old hunched-up tiny woman, wrapped in what looked like an old curtain. For a moment which seemed like an hour she looked at the two girls with beady black eyes and the girls stared back. Then she jumped to her feet in a very non-old-woman way and trotted towards them.

'Welcome, strangers,' she said and her voice sounded like rooks cawing. When she was standing up she seemed even smaller, not even as tall as Pen who was smaller than Jan. She was covered with a million wrinkles and she smelt of bonfires and seaweed. 'Welcome to yesterday and tomorrow and today's blackberry tea.' She scuttled back to the fire and stirred the pot with a wooden ladle, raising it high to let the blackberries plop back into the purplish liquid. 'Honey and berries for explorers to drink,' she said and Pen noticed that there were three tin mugs already standing in the embers. 'Sit on the bench and let me look for some books.'

Afterwards, days later, Pen and Jan couldn't decide how long they had been there. All they remembered was that they drank the blackberry and honey tea, which was a bit odd-tasting but nice, and that the old woman had brought out maps and picture books and a tin trunk with strange silver bracelets and necklaces and, most odd of all, a whole biscuit tin of pebbles, all beautifully painted. There were pebbles with fishes whose scales were coloured gold, pebbles with flowers and birds; there were tiny pictures of people's faces, Chinese writing, miniature maps, animals from Africa, a crown and the moon and stars.

'I toss 'em in the water and lay 'em on the beaches,' cawed the ancient one. 'I drop 'em by the roadside and hide 'em in the roots of trees. Them be my messages.' And she chortled and rubbed her little gnarled hands together and Pen noticed that her knobbly old fingers were splotched with paint.

'They're beautiful,' said Jan, her eyes wide in her red face, 'you are clever.' But the old one was staring past them to the shore.

'The boy,' she whispered, and Pen jumped to her feet and strained her eyes across the lake to see the jetty. She could just make out Jacko at the water's edge, slowly climbing over the rocks towards the part where no one was allowed to go. Pen's heart thudded in her throat.

'Jacko!' she yelled. 'Go back! Go back!' But he didn't hear. The little distant figure clambered up onto the

Smooth Rock, treacherously slippery; he stood there for a second, then suddenly he was gone.

'Jacko!' screamed Pen and she began to run down to the beach where the rowing boat lay on its side. 'Jacko!' and she tried to push the boat towards the water. Then something happened that Pen and Jan never quite forgot, nor ever quite remembered. Running like a crab, the old crone pushed past Pen, dragged the boat into the water and, standing in the prow, she started to row at top speed across the lake, using the oars back to front like a gondolier.

In the twilight the girls saw the skimming boat going so fast you would have thought it was a motor boat; then it reached Smooth Rock and they couldn't quite make out how it happened, but Jacko was in the boat. The boat came back towards the island, but now not so fast and what was very odd was that the crone looked very tall and not old a bit; and then Jacko (or was it Jacko?) took the oars, standing like a gondolier, only he was as tall as a grown man and together these two tall young people rowed back at a leisurely speed and Pen and Jan heard them laughing and talking and it didn't sound like Jacko and the crone.

Then all the rooks in the island tree (who hadn't been there before) set up a great cawing and flapping which made the girls look round: and when they looked back the crone was helping little wet Jacko out of the boat and they all set about kissing him and drying him by the fire, whose orange embers gleamed in the blue evening air.

'We must go,' said Pen in great agitation. 'Thank you for a lovely tea and for . . . ' she couldn't finish the sentence but the old woman's beady boot-button eyes crinkled kindly. They ran down to the boat. Pen and Jan rowed as they'd never rowed before and Jacko sat looking out at the lake, singing one of his home-made songs. When they got to the jetty it was dark and the island was lost in the lake mist.

That night Pen lay in bed with her door open, listening to her parents talking and to Jacko's sleeping sounds next door. She stared at the luminous stars she had stuck on her ceiling and thought she would never know a feeling more dreadful than thinking Jacko had drowned. She tiptoed into his room. It was tremendously untidy as usual and she trod on a fire engine he was building out of Lego, which made her hop about, biting her lips. In the darkness she could just make out his sleeping shape. He had pushed the sheets back and lay as if he had been thrown off a haystack. Pen pulled up the sheets very gently and prised open his pudgy fingers to put the treasure away safely. It was something round: a pebble.

She took it to the window and twitched the curtain back a bit so the moonlight fell on it. It was one of the old woman's painted stones – on one side was a painting of a beautiful face with long yellowish hair and dark black eyes and on the other side in tiny letters was written: *Keep me till we meet again.* She stood looking at it for a long minute then tiptoed across to where Jacko kept his rattling stone tin. She opened it and in the moonlight she saw them shining: flowers, fish, maps of India, trees, faces and a crown. They smelt faintly of woodsmoke and seaweed.

The next day the island had gone. Pen, being an honest girl, had tried to tell her parents about their adventures and Jacko's terrifying time nearly being drowned; but now there was no island and no old woman, and Jacko had been bone-dry and happy when they'd got back for supper. Her parents just smiled and pretended to be amazed but they thought Pen was inventing it. Jacko didn't help much either, doing his submarine-surfacing impression, and by lunchtime Pen began to think she'd dreamed it. Then she remembered Jacko's stone tin.

'Jacko, show your lovely pebbles to Mum. Show them, Jacko.'

Obediently Jacko took the tin from under the kitchen radiator where he had stowed it for safety that morning. It was full of smooth, plain, dull, ordinary pebbles, not painted or pretty or anything.

'Lovely, dear,' said Mum, and went outside to get some Brussels sprouts. Pen took Jacko by the shoulders and pinched her fingers tightly round his bones, not to hurt him, but to show she meant business.

'I saw them!' she hissed. 'I saw all the faces, animals and maps, and I saw the stone you were holding last night in bed. It said: *Keep me till we meet again.* What did that mean, Jacko? You must tell me,' and she tightened her grip and scowled right into his babyish face.

Jacko made a chimp mouth but then thought better of it. He closed his eyes as though he was trying to remember something difficult. Then he opened them and whispered, 'Nineteen!'

'Nineteen!' whispered Pen. 'Nineteen what? Nineteen ninety-six? Nineteen miles away? Nineteen what, Jacko?' And she shook him. He wriggled free.

'Just nineteen, silly,' he said and grinned. 'When I'm nineteen. She's coming back when I'm nineteen.'

HECTOR'S GREAT ESCAPE
Bel Mooney

Illustrated by Anthony Kerins

'I hate the smell!' said Sam, wrinkling up his nose.

'But it smells like the country, love,' said Sam's mum, as she unpacked the last box, and stored her best glasses away in a cupboard.

'Well then, I don't like the country,' muttered Sam.

'You have to give it a chance,' said his mum, frowning. 'That smell's just the silage from the farm, and a good healthy smell it is too.'

'All I can smell is cows' poo,' said Sam, 'and I think it's gross!' Then he ran out of the kitchen and into the small sitting room, where he switched on the television.

But Sam wasn't really watching the programme. All he could think about was how unhappy he was, and that it just wasn't fair. Ten days ago they had moved from the city, where he was born and which he liked – to this little village in the middle of nowhere. His parents said the cottage – and Dad's new job in the small town near by, and the village school for Sam – was everything they had always wanted.

'A dream come true,' said Mum.

'More like a nightmare,' snapped Sam, 'and I wish I could wake up and be back home.'

'This *is* home, love,' said Mum.

'You'll settle down, Sammy,' smiled Dad.

'But all the other children, they talk in a funny way,' wailed Sam.

'Just a country accent,' said Dad, 'and you'll get used to it. You'll get used to everything soon, old son. Just wait and see.'

Two weeks later, Sam was still waiting. The truth was, he didn't believe it could ever come right. He missed his best friends Robert and Kevin, and the sound of the traffic, and the shops just down the road that stayed open until late, and even the park with its wide paths and playground. He missed the sense of people all round, and the glow of city lights. He longed to be back where he belonged.

Not here. Here there were fields, fields, fields. There was no bus from the village, and not even one shop to buy sweets from. It was autumn and the rain dripped from tall trees which Sam couldn't name. The lane was muddy, and he hated always having to pull on his boots to go outside. It was much too quiet – that is, apart from the noises that came from Mr Foster's farm, not far away. Sometimes the lane was crowded with cows on their way from one field to another, and Sam hated the large, clumsy black and white beasts, with dirty legs and tails. They were so different from the pictures of farm animals you saw in books: fluffy white sheep and smooth, clean brown cows. These scruffy cows and sheep were real enough – you could smell that. And they *looked* at you with cold little eyes, as if they could tell you were actually afraid of them – though, of course, that was a secret. Sometimes it was as if they *knew* – those stupid, dumb animals – that you didn't belong.

At least, that was what Sam felt.

He was so lonely too – all the time. The children in his class tried to be friendly, but Sam felt so strange. He sounded different and he looked different and he liked different things. Afraid of getting things wrong, he hardly spoke. So the other children thought him a stuck-up city kid, and gave up trying to bother with him. Sam thought it could never come right. He lay awake at night and dreamed about running away, back to the city. 'I could live with Kevin, or Rob,' he muttered. He told himself that the only thing that stopped him was the thought of upsetting Mum and Dad.

One Saturday, about four weeks after their move, the sun was shining, and Sam's parents got very excited.

'Let's go for a long walk!' said Dad.

'Don't want to,' muttered Sam.

'We could explore that wood across the valley,' said Mum, rummaging in the drawer for her gloves.

'It looks spooky,' shivered Sam.

They set off, with Sam lagging behind from the beginning. No matter how much his parents laughed and tried to make him join in, and pointed out trees and birds – he sulked. He said he was tired, he said he was bored, he said the fields were too muddy, he said his legs ached . . . and at last he got his reward. Mum looked sad and Dad looked cross, and the sun disappeared from the sky.

'Why on earth are you being like this?' shouted Dad, when at last they arrived back at the cottage.

'BECAUSE I DON'T LIKE IT HERE!' yelled Sam, as he rushed upstairs and slammed his bedroom door behind him.

The room seemed so tiny, much smaller than his old bedroom. Sam knew he couldn't go downstairs because, to tell the truth, he was ashamed of himself for spoiling Mum's day. This is like being in a prison, he thought unhappily.

After a few moments he went to the window, rested his elbows on the sill, and looked out. There was a small paddock opposite the cottage, dotted with apple trees. It had been empty since they had moved. But as Sam watched, he noticed a flicker of something white in the corner of the field, hidden by the hedge.

He stared, thinking of ghosts for one wild scary second. But he knew that was silly. *If* there was such a thing as a ghost it would only come out at night, not flit about a field in broad daylight. So what was in the paddock?

As he stared, the thing trotted from its corner at last, and into full view. It was a very large sheep, or so Sam thought. It ran into the middle of the paddock, then all round the edge, then back into the middle, then back against the hedges, as if looking for something. Or desperately trying to find a way out. Something about the animal made Sam feel sorry for it.

It looks . . . lonely, he thought. It looks as if it's in prison too.

In a flash Sam ran down the stairs, pulled on his boots in the porch, and crossed the lane to the paddock gate. To his amazement the creature trotted over immediately to see him, and although Sam knew very little about animals, he knew enough to realise that this was not a sheep. It was a ram, with curling horns.

He stared at the ram and the ram stared back at him.

Then, very slowly – and feeling rather nervous of those horns – Sam put out his hand. Immediately the animal started back.

'You're scared of *me!*' whispered Sam. 'Don't be afraid, I won't hurt you.'

As he watched, the ram ducked and pulled at a tuft of grass, chewing it round and round in a comical way. Sam laughed.

'You look like you're chewing gum,' he said.

The ram finished his mouthful and looked at Sam, as if it wanted to ask him a question. 'You're hungry, aren't you?' said Sam.

Without thinking, he bent down and tore up a handful of juicy, long green grass from beneath the hedge near by. He offered it to the ram, pulling back his hand quickly as the chomping jaws took the delicious grass and chewed and chewed. Sam laughed again.

'Oh, he's a greedy lad, this one,' said a voice behind him, making Sam jump.

He turned, and there was Mr Foster, the farmer, standing with a broad grin on his face and a bucket in his hand.

'You're the new lad, aren't you? From Sunnybank Cottage? How do you like our village then?'

'Er, it's lovely,' said Sam.

'And what do you think of our big Hector?' Mr Foster pointed at the ram.

'He's . . . very nice,' said Sam, politely.

'I expect my sheep'll think that, when I put him with them,' winked Mr Foster. 'But that won't be for a few weeks yet, or else I'll be having the lambing too early.'

Sam nodded wisely, as if he understood.

'So we've got to keep Hector happy,' said Mr Foster. 'You want to help me feed him? He's got to keep his strength up!'

He unfastened the gate, and went quickly into the paddock, waiting briefly for Sam to follow him, before pushing the gate closed once more.

'Have to watch him,' the farmer explained. 'Give him half a chance and he'll be off up that lane looking for his girlfriends!'

Sam had never before been in a field with a farm animal. It made him feel rather excited, but just a bit nervous. Not that Hector was anywhere near. As soon as they walked in he backed off and ran about ten metres away.

'You want to give him his dinner?' asked Mr Foster, shaking the bucket.

'Doesn't he eat grass?' asked Sam.

'Not enough for him! He has these sheep nuts as well,' explained the farmer, passing Sam the bucket.

As soon as Sam rattled some into the old sink that served as a trough, the ram came trotting over without any fear, and started to munch.

'He loves them!' cried Sam, delighted, as if he had made the food himself.

He reached out and stroked Hector's head as he ate. The wool was tightly curled, and felt springy. As he bent down Sam caught a warm, damp, oily smell, which was much nicer than he expected.

'You an' him – you can be mates,' smiled Mr Foster.

The next morning Sam went out to see Hector, and gave him some grass. He spent a long time watching the ram run around the orchard, and when he went home he found himself staring from the window too. When he saw the farmer coming along the lane with the bucket of food, he ran down and asked if he could feed Hector.

'You can feed him every day if you like. One less job for me, lad,' smiled Mr Foster.

From then on each day had a routine. As he walked to the village school, passing the paddock, Sam stopped to give the ram five or six handfuls of juicy long grass – because the ground was getting all muddy where Hector paced to and fro, to and fro, wishing he could get out. After school Sam went down to the farmyard, soon getting used to the snuffling and rustling of the cattle in their big shed, their heads poking out between the bars. Mr Foster had shown him the bin where the sheep nuts were kept, and Sam knew just how much to scoop into the bucket and take up to the ram.

'There you are, old boy,' he whispered, as Hector tucked into his supper, not noticing that Sam was scratching his woolly head. Again he would breathe in that sharp smell of damp oily wool and as the days passed he began to like it more and more. The more familar it grew, the better it comforted him, somehow. It coated his lungs and made him feel at home.

What's more, the ram trusted him. It was the first time in Sam's life that he had got to know an animal like this. The big, soft creature *needed* him, and the thought made Sam feel very happy, in a completely new way.

The trouble was, Hector didn't feel at home. When Sam looked out of his bedroom window, as it grew dark, he saw the ram running round and round the paddock, sometimes throwing himself against the tangled hedge. He looked bored and lonely. Sometimes Sam would wake in the middle of the night, and lie listening to the wind and the rain, imagining Hector out there on his own, feeling miserable.

'That's you putting yourself in his place, silly,' scoffed Dad. 'But animals don't think like us.'

'How do you *know?*' asked Sam.

'He doesn't,' Mum smiled.

'Well, I know Hector's fed up with being in that

paddock,' said Sam, feeling very grown up. 'He wants to be with a flock. That's what he needs. But he can't go with his girlfriends yet because we'll have the lambing too early, you see?'

Mum and Dad exchanged looks, then both started laughing. But Sam didn't mind. He knew it was really because they were pleased.

One chilly morning soon after that Sam woke up early, and looked out as usual. He stared and stared, but could not see Hector in the paddock. There was no doubt about it. Worse, Sam was sure there was a ragged hole in the old hedge, just near the gate.

Oh no! he thought.

He knew, as he reached the paddock gate, that Hector was gone. The gap in the hedge told its own story: the ram had pushed and pushed during the night, and finally broken through. But where was he now? And what should Sam do?

He ran down the lane to the farmhouse, to look for Mr Foster. But Mrs Foster opened the kitchen door and said he was already out working in one of the farthest fields, mending the electric fence. She smiled at Sam, and ruffled his hair. 'Don't worry, my love. I'll go over and get him and keep a lookout for that old ram along the lane on the way. You go to school now, and thanks for your trouble.'

The trouble was, Sam didn't like being sent away like that. After all, if Hector was his pet everyone would expect him to be worried, not just go to school as if nothing had happened. And Hector *was* his pet. Didn't he feed him every day?

Sam's cottage was right in the middle of the village, and at the top of the little lane outside the front door there was a bigger lane that led two ways. If you turned left you went along for two miles to the next village. That was the direction Mr Foster's land lay, and so the way Mrs Foster would drive. But if you turned right, after about five hundred metres you came to the big main road. Lorries rushed along this road, and lots of cars, usually going very fast.

Sam closed his eyes because a terrible picture suddenly flashed across his brain. He imagined Hector going as far as the main road, then feeling afraid, then somebody trying to catch him, then running out into the traffic. He heard the scream of brakes . . . and 'saw' Hector's body lying there.

'Oh *no!*' whispered Sam, feeling his hair prickle at the thought.

He knew if he went home Mum would fuss about breakfast and school, and he wouldn't have the chance to catch Hector. But . . . *how* would he catch Hector? He thought for a moment, then made his plan. . .

About ten minutes later Sam was running up the lane, and turning right at the top. He jogged along, his heart beating quickly, and glancing into each garden as he passed, in case Hector had been sidetracked by the sight of somebody's tasty lawn. But there was no sign of the ram, and the hum of the heavy morning traffic came nearer and nearer. Sam had an awful cold feeling inside him. Somehow he just *knew* that Mr and Mrs Foster wouldn't find the ram in the other direction.

The main road was only a short way away now. Lorries roared past – and right at the edge of the road Sam saw that familiar bulky shape. Hector was frightened. He shook his head from side to side, and made little runs, as if he didn't know what to do. Just then someone came along the narrow pavement by the hedge at the side of the road. It was a man Sam had seen in the village.

He's trying to catch him, thought Sam, but that's no good . . .

Sure enough, Hector panicked. He started to run – out into the traffic. Sam screamed, but nobody heard. He closed his eyes for a second, waiting for the screech, followed by a thud. But luckily Hector had just managed to find a gap, so that when Sam opened his eyes again the animal was standing on the narrow grassy central strip, with cars passing on each side. He looked very frightened.

He won't be so lucky a second time, thought Sam.

Slowly he walked forward. The man who had frightened the ram was standing there, looking worried.

'He could cause a nasty accident,' he said, shaking his head.

'Hector could get killed!' said Sam.

He just knew that he was the only person who could save Hector. 'You stay there,' he said to the man, 'because if anybody goes near him he'll panic again.' Then Sam looked right, then left, then right again and, seeing a gap in the traffic, walked quickly forward, making little soothing noises as he did each day when he fed the ram. As he walked he rummaged in the deep pockets of his anorak.

He stopped at the edge of the grassy strip, about two metres from Hector. In one hand he held the round plastic scoop he used to fill the bucket with sheep nuts from the bin. With the other hand he scooped the loose food from his pocket. When the plastic scoop was full he held it out to Hector.

'Come on, old boy, come on! It's breakfast time,' he said, in a soft voice.

Hector looked and sniffed. For a moment he didn't move, but he knew the boy, and the food smelled good – so he took a step forward, then another. Sam allowed him to get very near, before starting to move back. He held his free hand up towards the traffic, hoping that the man would help stop it. He did.

The cars stopped, and people smiled as the boy moved slowly back across the road, never taking his eyes off Hector, and holding out the delicious bait. The ram trotted after him, not noticing anything but his breakfast. Back along the village street they went, and when Sam noticed Mr and Mrs Foster walking quickly towards him, together with Mum, he held up his hand to stop them, just as he had done the traffic. Nothing must break the spell between the ram and himself. For the first time in his life Sam felt in charge.

Sam led Hector right into his paddock, then he put down the food so the ram could gobble it up. A relieved Mr Foster shut the gate behind them.

'You're a clever lad,' said the farmer.

'I'll say!' said Mrs Foster.

'You'll be late for school,' smiled Mum, who was feeling very proud.

'Won't Hector get out again?' was all Sam said, looking at Mr Foster.

'Don't you worry, Sam. I'll fence off that hole before you can say Rambo,' said Mr Foster with a grin. 'And in a day or two you can help me get this old boy into the trailer, and across to the sheep.'

'Yes, and you wait till lambing time,' said Mrs Foster. 'Would you like to help with that? You'll love it. I think you're a born shepherd,'

Sam nodded happily. The birds were singing in the trees all around. Crisp autumn leaves shone gold and red in the sunlight. Everything smelt fresh and healthy. He went over to Hector, who still had his nose buried in the plastic scoop, looking for the last of the sheep nuts.

To the farmer's amazement, the ram let the boy kneel down and wrap his arms around the thick woolly neck.

'Don't run away again, Hector,' whispered Sam. 'It's much more fun staying here.'

MUCK AND MAGIC
Michael Morpurgo

Illustrated by Elizabeth Frink

I am sometimes asked these days how I got started. I should love to be able to say that it was all because I had some dream, some vision, or maybe that I just studied very hard. None of this would really be true. I owe what I am, what I have become, what I do each day of my life, to a bicycle ride I took a long time ago now, when I was twelve years old and also to a pile of muck, horse muck.

The bike was new that Christmas. It was maroon, and I remember it was called a Raleigh Wayfarer. It had all you could ever dream of in a bike – in those days. It had a bell, a dynamo lamp front and rear, five gears and a silver pump. I loved it instantly and spent every hour I could out riding it. And when I wasn't riding it, I was polishing it.

We lived on the edge of town, so it was easy to ride off down Mill Lane past the estate, along the back of the soap factory where my father worked, when he did work, and then out into the countryside beyond. It was too far to walk, and in a car you zoomed past so fast that the cows and the trees were only ever brief, blurred memories. On my bike I was close to everything for the first time. I felt the cold and the rain on my face. I mooed at the cows, and they looked up and blinked at me lazily. I shouted at the crows and watched them lift off cawing and croaking into the wind. But best of all, no one knew where I was – and that included me sometimes. I was always getting myself lost and coming back at dusk, late. I would brace myself for all the sighing and tutting and ticking off that inevitably followed. I bore it all stoically because they didn't really mean it, and anyway it had all been worth it. I'd had a taste of real freedom and I wanted more of it.

After a while I discovered the circuit that seemed to be just about ideal. It was a two-hour run, not too many hills going up, plenty going down, a winding country lane that criss-crossed a river past narrow cottages where hardly anyone seemed to live, under the shadow of a church where sometimes I stopped and put flowers on the graves that everyone else seemed to have forgotten, and then along the three-barred iron fence where the horses always galloped over to see me, their tails and heads high, their ears pricked.

There were three of them: a massive bay hunter that looked down on me from a great height, a chubby little pony with a face like a chipmunk, and a fine-boned grey that flowed and floated over the ground with such grace and ease that I felt like clapping every time I saw her move. She made me laugh too because she often made rude, farty noises as she came trotting over to see me. I called her Peg after a flying horse called Pegasus that I'd read about in a book. The small one I called Chip, and the great bay, Big Boy. I'd cuddle them all, give each of them a sugar lump – two for Peg because she wasn't as pushy as the other two – told them my troubles, cuddled them a little more and went on my way, always reluctantly.

I hated to leave them because I was on the way back home after that, back to homework, and the sameness of the house, and my mother's harassed scurrying and my little brother's endless tantrums. I lay in my room and dreamed of those horses, of Peg in particular. I pictured myself riding her bareback through flowery meadows, up rutty mountain passes, fording rushing streams where she'd stop to drink. I go to sleep at nights lying down on the straw with her, my head resting on her warm belly. But when I woke her belly was always my pillow, and my father was in the bathroom next door, gargling and spitting into the sink, and there was school to face, again. But after school I'd be away on my bike and that was all that mattered to me. I gave up ballet lessons on Tuesdays. I gave up cello lessons Fridays. I never missed a single day, no matter what the weather – rain, sleet, hail – I simply rode through it all, living for the moment when Peg would rest her heavy head on my shoulder and I'd hear that sugar lump crunching inside her grinding jaw.

It was Spring. I know that because there were

daffodils all along the grass verge by the fence, and there was nowhere to lie my bike down on the ground without squashing them. So I leaned it up against the fence and fished in my pocket for the sugar lumps. Chip came scampering over as he always did, and Big Boy wandered lazily up behind him, his tail flicking nonchalantly. But I saw no sign of Peg. When Big Boy had finished his sugar lump, he started chewing at the saddle of my bike and knocked it over. I was just picking it up when I saw her coming across the field towards me. She wore long green boots and a jersey covered in planets and stars, gold against the dark, deep blue of space. But what struck me most was her hair, the wild white curly mop of it, around her face that was somehow both old and young at the same time.

'Who are you?' she asked. It was just a straight question, not a challenge.

'Bonnie,' I replied.

'She's not here,' said the woman.

'Where is she?'

'It's the spring grass. I have to keep her inside from now on.'

'Why?'

'Laminitis. She's fine all through the winter, eats all the grass she likes no trouble. But she's only got to sniff the spring grass and it comes back. It heats the hoof, makes her lame.' She waved away the two horses and came closer, scrutinising me. 'I've seen you before, haven't I? You like horses, don't you?' I smiled 'Me too,' she went on. 'But they're a lot of work.'

'Work?' I didn't understand.

'Bring them in, put them out, groom them, pick out their feet, feed them, muck them out. I'm not as young as I was, Bonnie. You don't want a job do you, in the stables? Be a big help. The grey needs a good long walk every day, and a good mucking out. Three pounds an hour, what do you say?'

Just like that. I said yes, of course. I could come evenings and weekends.

'I'll see you tomorrow then,' she said. 'You'll need wellies. I've got some that should fit. You be careful on the roads now.' And she turned and walked away.

I cycled home that day singing my heart out and high as a kite. It was my first paying job, and I'd be looking after Peg. It really was a dream come true.

I didn't tell anyone at home, nor at school. Where I went on my bike, what I did, was my own business, no one else's. Besides there was always the chance that father would stop me – you never knew with him. And I certainly didn't want any of my school friends oaring in on this. At least two of them knew all about horses, or they said they did, and I knew they would never stop telling me the right way to do this or that. Best just to keep everything to myself.

To get to the house the next day – you couldn't see it from the road – I cycled up a long drive through high trees that whispered at me. I had to weave around the pot-holes, bump over sleeping policemen, but then came out on to a smooth tarmac lane where I could freewheel downhill and hear the comforting tic-a-tic of my wheels beneath me.

I nearly came off when I first saw them. Everywhere in amongst the trees there were animals, but none of them moved. They just looked at me. There were wild boar, dogs, horses, and gigantic men running through trees like hunters. But all were still as statues. Then I saw the stables on my right, Peg looking out at me, ears pricked and shaking her mane; and beyond the stables was a long house of flint and brick with a tiled roof, and a clock tower with doves fluttering around it.

The stable block was deserted. I didn't like to call out, so I opened the gate and went over to Peg and stroked her nose. That was when I noticed a pair of wellies waiting by the door, and slipped into one of them was a piece of paper. I took it out and read:

Hope these fit. Take her for a walk down the tracks, not in the fields. She can nibble the grass, but not too much. Then muck out the stables. Save what dry straw you can – it's expensive. When you've done, shake out half a bale in her stable – you'll find straw and hay in the barn. She has two slices of hay in her rack. Don't forget to fill up the water buckets.

It was not signed.

Until then I had not given it a single thought, but I had never led a horse or ridden a horse in all my life. Come to that, I hadn't mucked out a stable either. Peg had a halter on her already, and a rope hung from a hook beside the stable. I put the wellies on – they were only a little too big – clipped on the rope, opened the stable door and led her out, hoping, praying she would behave. I need not have worried. It was Peg that took me for a walk. I simply stopped whenever she did, let her nibble for a while, and then asked her gently if it wasn't time to move on. She knew the way, up the track through the woods, past the running men and the wild boar, then forking off down past the ponds where a bronze water buffalo drank without ever moving his lips. White fish glided ghostly under the shadow of his nose. The path led upwards from there and passed a hen house where a solitary goose stretched his neck, flapped his wings and honked at us. Peg stopped for a moment, lifted her nose and wrinkled it at the goose who began preening himself busily. After a while I found myself coming back to the stable-yard gate and Peg led me in. I tied her up in the yard and set about mucking out the stables.

I was emptying the wheelbarrow onto the muck heap when I felt someone behind me. I turned round. She was older than I remembered her, greyer in the face, and more frail. She was dressed in jeans and a rough sweater this time, and seemed to be covered in white powder, as if someone had thrown flour at her. Even her cheeks were smudged with it. She glowed when she smiled.

'Where's there's muck there's money, that's what they say,' she laughed; and then she shook her head. 'Not true, I'm afraid, Bonnie. Where there's muck, there's magic. Now that's true.' I wasn't sure what she meant by that. 'Horse muck,' she went on by way of explanation. 'Best magic in the world for vegetables. I've got leeks in my garden longer than, longer than . . .' She looked around her. 'Twice as long as your bicycle pump. All the soil asks is that we feed it with that stuff, and it'll do anything we want it to. It's like anything, Bonnie, you have to put in more than you take out. You want some tea when you've finished?'

'Yes please.'

'Come up to the house then. You can have your money.' She laughed at that. 'Maybe there is money in muck after all.'

As I watched her walk away, a small yappy dog came bustling across the lawn, ran at her and sprang into her arms. She cradled him, put him over her shoulder and disappeared into the house.

I finished mucking out the stable as quickly as I could, shook out some fresh straw, filled up the water buckets and led Peg back in. I gave her a goodbye kiss on the nose and rode my bike up to the house.

I found her in the kitchen, cutting bread.

'I've got peanut butter or honey,' she said. I didn't like either, but I didn't say so.

'Honey,' I said. She carried the mugs of tea, and I carried the plate of sandwiches. I followed her out across a cobbled courtyard, accompanied by the yappy dog, down some steps and into a great glass building where there stood a gigantic white horse. The floor was covered in newspaper, and everywhere was crunchy underfoot with plaster. The shelves all around were full of heads and arms and legs and hands. A white sculpture of a dog stood guard over the plate of sandwiches and never even sniffed them. She sipped her tea between her hands and looked up at the giant horse. The horse looked just like Peg, only a lot bigger.

'It's no good,' she sighed. 'She needs a rider.' She turned to me suddenly. 'You wouldn't be the rider, would you?' she asked.

'I can't ride.'

'You wouldn't have to, not really. You'd just sit there, that's all, and I'd sketch you.'

'What, now?'

'Why not? After tea be all right?'

And so I found myself sitting astride Peg that same afternoon in the stable yard. She was tied up by her rope, pulling contentedly at her hay net and paying no attention to us whatsoever. It felt strange up there, with Peg shifting warm underneath me. There was no saddle, and she asked me to hold the reins one-handed, loosely, to feel 'I was part of the horse'. The worst of it was that I was hot, stifling hot, because she had dressed me up as an Arab. I had great swathes of cloth over and around my head and I was draped to my feet with a long

heavy robe so that nothing could be seen of my jeans or sweater or wellies.

'I never told you my name, did I?' said the lady, sketching furiously on a huge pad. 'That was rude of me. I'm Liza. When you come tomorrow, you can give me a hand making you if you like. I'm not as strong as I was, and I'm in a hurry to get on with this. You can mix the plaster for me. Would you like that?' Peg snorted and pawed the ground. 'I'll take that as a yes, shall I?' She laughed, and walked around behind the horse, turning the page of her sketch pad. 'I want to do one more from this side and one from the front, then you can go home.'

Half an hour later when she let me down and unwrapped me, my bottom was stiff and sore.

'Can I see?' I asked her.

'I'll show you tomorrow,' she said. 'You will come, won't you?' She knew I would, and I did.

I came every day after that to muck out the stables and to walk Peg, but what I looked forward to most – even more than being with Peg – was mixing up Liza's plaster for her in the bucket, climbing the stepladder with it, watching her lay the strips of cloth dunked in the wet plaster over the frame of the rider, building me up from the iron skeleton of wire, to what looked at first like an Egyptian mummy, then a riding Arab at one with his horse, his robes shrouding him with mystery. I knew all the while it was me in that skeleton, me inside that mummy. I was the Arab sitting astride his horse looking out over the desert. She worked ceaselessly, and with such a fierce determination that I didn't like to interrupt. We were joined together by a common, comfortable silence.

At the end of a month or so we stood back, the two of us, and looked up at the horse and rider, finished.

'Well,' said Liza, her hands on her hips. 'What do you think, Bonnie?'

'I wish,' I whispered, touching the tail of the horse, 'I just wish I could do it.'

'But you did do it, Bonnie,' she said and I felt her hand on my shoulder. 'We did it together. I couldn't have done it without you.' She was a little breathless as she spoke. 'Without you, that horse would never have had a rider. I'd never have thought of it. Without you mixing my plaster, holding the bucket, I couldn't have done it.' Her hand gripped me tighter. 'Do you want to do one of your own?'

'I can't.'

'Of course you can. But you have to look around you first, not just glance, but really look. You have to breathe it in, become a part of it, feel that you're a part of it. You draw what you see, what you feel. Then you make what you've drawn. Use clay if you like, or do what I do and build up plaster over a wire frame. Then set to work with your chisel, just like I do, until it's how you want it. If I can do it, you can do it. I tell you what. You can have a corner of my studio if you like, just so long as you don't talk when I'm working. How's that?'

So my joyous spring blossomed into a wonderful

summer. After a while, I even dared to ride Peg bareback sometimes on the way back to the stable yard; and I never forgot what Liza told me. I looked about me. I listened. And the more I listened and the more I looked, the more I felt at home in this new world. I became a creature of the place. I belonged there as much as the wren that sang at me high on the vegetable garden wall, as much as the green dragonfly hovering over the pool by the water buffalo. I sketched Peg. I sketched Big Boy (I couldn't sketch Chip – he just came out round). I bent my wire frames into shape and I began to build my first horse sculpture, layer on layer of strips of cloth dunked in plaster just like Liza did. I moulded them into shape around the frame, and when they dried I chipped away and sanded. But I was never happy with what I'd done.

All this time, Liza worked on beside me in the studio, and harder, faster, more intensely than ever. I helped her whenever she asked me, too, mixing, holding the bucket for her, just as I had done before.

It was a Rising Christ, she said, Christ rising from the dead, his face strong, yet gentle too, immortal it seemed; but his body, vulnerable and mortal. From time to time she'd come over and look at my stumpy effort that looked as much like a dog as a horse to me, and she would walk around it nodding her approval. 'Coming on, coming on,' she'd say. 'Maybe just a little bit off here perhaps.' And she'd chisel away for a minute or two, and a neck or leg would come to sudden life. I told her once, 'It's like magic.' She thought for a moment, and said; 'That's exactly what it is, Bonnie. It's a God-given thing, a God-given magic, and it's not to be wasted. Don't waste it, Bonnie. Don't ever waste it.'

The horse and rider came back from the foundry, bronze now and magnificent. I marvelled at it. It stood outside her studio, and when it caught the red of the evening sun, I could scarcely take my eyes off it. But these days Liza seemed to tire more easily, and she would sit longer over her tea, gazing out at her horse and rider.

'I am so pleased with that, Bonnie,' she said, 'so pleased we did it together.'

The Christ figure was finished and went off to the foundry a few weeks before I had to go on my summer holiday. 'By the time you come back again,' said Liza, 'it should be back. It's going to hang above the door of the village church. Isn't that nice? It'll be there for ever. Well, not for ever. Nothing is for ever.'

The holiday was in Cornwall. We stayed where we always did, in Cadgwith, and I drew every day. I drew boats and gulls and lobster pots. I made sculptures with wet sand – sleeping giants, turtles, whales – and everyone thought I was mad not to go swimming and boating. The sun shone for fourteen days. I never had such a perfect holiday, even though I didn't have my bike, or Peg or Liza with me.

My first day back, the day before school began, I cycled out to Liza's place with my best boat drawing in a stiff envelope under my sweater. The stable yard was deserted. There were no horses in the fields. Peg wasn't in her stable and I could find no one up at the house, no Liza, no yappy dog. I stopped in the village to ask but there was no one about. It was like a ghost village. Then the church bell began to ring. I leaned my bike up against the churchyard wall and ran up the path. There was Liza's Rising Christ glowing in the sun above the doorway, and inside they were singing hymns.

I crept in, lifting the latch carefully so that I wouldn't be noticed. The hymn was just finishing. Everyone was sitting down and coughing. I managed to squeeze myself in at the end of a pew and sat down too. The church was packed. A choir in red robes and white surplices sat on either side of the altar. The vicar was taking off his glasses and putting them away. I looked everywhere for Liza's wild white curls, but could not find her. It was difficult for me to see much over everyone's heads. Besides, some people were wearing hats, so I presumed she was too and stopped looking for her. She'd be there somewhere.

The vicar began. 'Today was to be a great day, a happy day for all of us. Liza was to unveil her Rising Christ above the south door. It was her gift to us, to all of us who live here, and to everyone who will come here to our church in the centuries to come. Well, as we all now know, there was no unveiling, because she wasn't here to do it. On Monday evening she watched her Rising Christ winched into place. She died the next day.'

Well I didn't hear anything else he said. It was only then that I saw the coffin resting on trestles between the pulpit and the lectern, with a single wreath of white flowers laid on it, only then that I took in the awful truth.

I didn't cry as the coffin passed right by me on its way out of the church. I suppose I was still trying to believe it. I stood and listened to the last prayers over the grave, numb inside, grieving as I had never grieved before or since, but still not crying. I waited until almost everyone had gone and went over to the grave. A man was taking off his jacket and hanging it on the branch of the tree. He spat on his hands, rubbed them and picked up his spade. He saw me. 'You family?' he said.

'Sort of,' I replied. I reached inside my sweater and pulled out the boat drawing from Cadgwith. 'Can you put it in?' I asked. 'It's a drawing. It's for Liza.'

'Course,' he said, and he took it from me. 'She'd like that. Fine lady, she was. The things she did with her hands. Magic, pure magic.'

It was just before Christmas the same year that a cardboard tube arrived in the post, addressed to me. I opened it in the secrecy of my room. A rolled letter fell out, typed and very short.

Dear Miss Mallet,

In her will, the late Liza Bonallack instructed us, her solicitors, to send you this drawing. We would ask you to keep us informed of any future changes of address.

With best wishes.

I unrolled it and spread it out. It was of me sitting on
Peg, swathed in Arab clothes. Underneath was written:

For dearest Bonnie,
  I never paid you for all that mucking out, did I? You
shall have this instead, and when you are twenty-one you
shall have the artist's copy of our horse and rider sculpture.
But by then you will be doing your own sculptures. I know
you will.
  God bless,
  Liza.

So here I am, nearly thirty now. And as I look out at the
settling snow from my studio, I see Liza's horse and
rider standing in my back garden; and all around, my
own sculptures gathered in silent homage.

Derek Dungbeetle
and the Lost Lover
Alick Rowe

Illustrated by Martin Chatterton

Grey day in the metropolis. Weather hard down and traffic dull in the distance. From my office I could hear the thousand sounds that make up life round Elm Plaza. Rain hit the roof and splashed down the window. It was a good grey day. The sort of day I like – but, hey, that's the way a dungbeetle is.

To tell you the truth, in spite of the day I wasn't feeling so good. Whether it was the liquor from the night before or the new insecticides I was one quiet dungbeetle. So when I heard the steps on the stairs I sighed and pulled my eyes from my pride and joy parked in the lot outside the block.

'You the investigator?'

She was not impressed. I pushed files off the chair and brushed it.

'That's what it says on the door. Derek Dungbeetle. Investigator.'

She slid gracefully onto the seat and modestly arranged four of her legs while I tried not to think about the other two. Her body was a soft red and she had great spots. She looked round and I wished I'd cleaned up the office. I took the chair behind the desk.

'What's on your mind?' I leaned back in my chair and waited for her to tell her story. When she'd finished she watched me through dark mysterious eyes.

It was the story every sleuth gets once in a while. The Missing Lover. I kept my eyes from the dame's legs and a thought crossed what was left of my mind.

'Why come to me? Missing persons are not my speciality. You could have gone to the bluebottles. You could have gone to a private fly.'

'I got your name from a friend.'

I had friends? I asked who.

'Milly.'

I relaxed. The millipede was all right. She was a reporter on the daily flypaper and we'd just cracked a tough crime together.

'You see,' she whispered, 'my Donald was . . .' Her eyes filled with tears but she pulled herself together. 'He was what you are,' she breathed. 'A dungbeetle.'

I whistled under my breath and reached for a toothpick to chew on. A love affair between a ladybird and a dungbeetle? Heavy. She read my thoughts, meticulously uncrossed her legs and stood.

'I've shocked you,' she murmured. 'I'm sorry. I thought you might understand.' She began moving to the door.

'Hey, lady,' I called. 'Listen. Nothing shocks me, OK? I'm a businessman. I sell my time and skills.' The ladybird looked steadily at me as she thought it over, then moved back to the chair and folded those luscious limbs while I looked for paper in the drawer to make notes.

It was late when we finished. Lights were blazing in the plaza and the traffic, louder than ever. I closed the file and leaned back.

'There's dungbeetles going missing every day,' I said carefully. 'Glow-worms too. Nobody knows why. There's a department at City Hall working on it right now. I don't promise you anything.'

She looked at me. 'I don't ask for promises. Like you say, you're a businessman. I'll buy your time and talent.'

We talked money. She was cute and she was smart but rich she was not. I heard myself agree a sum way below the usual fee. She thanked me and stood. 'Maybe there'll be some other way I can make it up to you, Mr Dungbeetle,' she said. She fluttered all her eyelids and I almost fell off the chair.

'Derek,' I said. 'My friends call me Derek.'

She smiled a small smile. 'Derek,' she muttered, trying the name for size. 'They call me Lady.'

'That figures. Where do I find you, Lady?'

She took a book of matches from her bag and tore off the cover. 'Call me at this number.' She closed her bag again. 'But make it early or make it late. I work evenings.' The door shut softly behind her, forgetting to creak and slam like it does with ordinary mortals.

From the window I watched her swing those superb spots across the plaza. This would not be easy. Donald was just another missing dungbeetle statistic in Department Z's ledger at City Hall. I turned out the light, locked the door and went out to the parking lot.

Sure every dungbeetle has his dung-roll. But there are rolls and there are rolls – and then there is the Copra Sports. The best. Mine. All my life I'd wanted a Copra and last year I'd finally made it. I moved the Copra smoothly out of the parking lot and into the plaza. I slid her into the stream of traffic heading west and thought about Lady as we bowled along.

I'd recognised the name on the cover on the book of matches before she'd torn it off. The Flea Pit. A small nightclub with a big reputation. I wondered how Lady fitted into it as I signalled left and filtered into the stream heading for Pine Square. I needed to talk to someone at City Hall.

The clerk in Department Z fussed and clicked importantly as he turned over the pages of his ledger. I put my face into neutral as I tried to think of one word to describe my feelings towards him. Repugnance – hey, that was a good one. The pratty little punk smiled over the ledger and – since I needed his help – I tried to forget

I did not like deathwatch beetles in general and this one in particular. I put my ideals into reverse and smiled so gruesomely back that a plant in the window groaned and died.

'Is that your Copra Sports in the lot?' he asked. 'You must be very proud of it.' I smiled again. The window behind the plant cracked in six places and misted over. The deathwatch beetle peered carefully at me. 'How may I help you?'

I peered carefully back. 'Missing dungbeetles?' I suggested.

The deathwatch slammed his ledger shut and slid it into a drawer. His antennae straightened like swords. 'All information is classified. All information is secret. It is half after six and this office is closed!' He rammed the drawer shut and locked it. Immediately a clock struck the half-hour. I tried not to be impressed as I stood.

The punk sneered. He began to tick mockingly. 'Drive safely home with your Copra, sir. Such a fast ball of dung for such a small insect!' That did it. I composed my features to inspire maximum fear the way Odonata the dragonfly taught me. I turned in the doorway.

'Don't get in my way, tick-head,' I said quietly. 'Or you'll find out just how fast.'

I kept my eyes on him for the exact seven-seconds dose. His eyes popped wide open, his antennae shivered uncontrollably and he rattled inside his thorax. 'See you again,' I said, smiling so gruesomely that as I closed the door behind me I heard the clock shriek and jump off the wall.

It was a quarter before midnight when I hit the club. I pushed my way across the dance floor to a table and ordered liquor. The Flea Pit. Like the name suggests, the joint was jumping.

The owner was at his table near his office. Tonight Big Daddy Longlegs was entertaining the Chief. He entertained the Chief every night. It paid him to keep in with the bluebottles. It paid the bluebottles to keep in with him too.

Daddy Longlegs. Millionaire, politician and night-club owner. Nobody knew where he came from but that's the way he liked it so that's the way it was.

The band stopped playing and the dance floor emptied. Just before the lights eased down I thought I saw the Department Z tick-head making for Daddy's table but I told myself that was crazy. Then the lights went down and the band struck up. A spotlight hit the stage and I gulped.

It was Lady – dressed to kill. Lady – smiling that cute half-smile and easing her way to the front of the stage while the place went wild. Four glow-worms swayed at her feet. The applause died. A tenor saxophone wailed. And Lady sang the blues.

> 'I woke up this mornin' – turned the radio on.
> I say I woke up this mornin' and yes I turned it on.
> I heard my house was on fire and all my children gone.'

She was sensational. The glow-worms swayed to the cool, cool music which wrapped itself round Lady's low velvet voice.

> 'I got those ladybird blues
> From the bad bad news.
> It's true.
>
> 'O yes, those ladybird blues
> Gonna make me choose
> Somebody new.'

Lady's eyes met mine. I read shock.

> 'So please someone come and help me.
> I don' know what to do.'

She slowly lowered her head and the wailing sax took up her long last note as the glow-worms moved off-stage and the spotlight cut out. Applause rocked the joint as the stage lights came up and there was Lady, smiling, bowing and waving to folks she knew. But not to me. She left the stage and made for Big Daddy's table where the Chief was standing, leering and clapping hard with all available limbs. One cool ladybird. I got up to go. After Lady's performance there could be nothing else. I signalled for the check and had happy thoughts of sleep.

I was still happy as I strolled down the back street to the Copra. That Lady. I tried not to think of her with Big Daddy and the Chief. The Copra was in the shadows waiting for me and Lady's song drifted like smoke through my brain.

> 'I got those ladybird blues
> From the bad bad news . . .'

It was bad news all right. There were dark shapes in the shadows but before I could do anything useful about them they did something painful about me. As I fought against the growing cloud of unconsciousness I heard ticking somewhere close. I wanted sleep but not this badly. I slept.

Life began again. I almost wished it hadn't. My whole body felt like it had been kicked by a heavyweight centipede. Hey, maybe it had. I forced myself to open my eyes.

Lady was looking down on me, worried. I tried to make a wisecrack like private eyes always do in this situation but inspiration was hard to find. I fought against the temptation to look blearily round and whisper 'Where am I?' like they do on television, which would have been gross.

'Where am I?' I whispered, looking blearily round.

'Ssssh,' murmured Lady, leaning close and adjusting the ice pack over my fevered brow which was becoming more fevered every bit closer she came. I lay back and sent down an order to the strength department for a double helping and seconds. It seemed to be a long time arriving but it finally came.

'How did I get here?'

'One of the glow-worms – Gloria – was out on the balcony getting some air. She saw what happened.'

'Did Gloria see *who* happened to me?'

Lady shook her head. 'They took your Copra,' she added nervously.

She was right to be nervous. 'They did what?' I shouted, getting to my feet, almost falling down again and finally getting my balance by hooking a few limbs round the hatstand.

Lady was worried. 'Listen, Derek,' she said. 'Nothing in the metropolis happens by accident. If you were beaten up and your Copra stolen then that's what Big Daddy wanted – and nobody fights Daddy Longlegs. I've already lost one friend.' She looked at me from beneath her lashes. 'And I don't aim to lose another. A good dungbeetle is hard to find,' she murmured. 'Forget Donald. The case is finished.'

'Lady,' I said, finishing my liquor, 'the case has only just begun.' I made for the door in spite of urgent telegrams from all parts of my body. 'Love me: love my Copra. Hate my Copra: hate me. OK. But *steal* my Copra –' I turned and smiled lopsidedly – 'and somebody better take out life insurance. Fast.'

I took a cab down to Cedar Avenue and rode the elevator up to the twelfth branch. I rang Pete's bell. He was a bird who owed me a favour. He was not pleased to see me but his eyes missed nothing and if anybody could tell me where my Copra was it was Pete. And he did.

Back at my apartment I called the precinct. I knew the bluebottle on duty – his father had been an old friend. Buzz was young and as innocent as any cop was ever going to be but I gave him the downtown address and he promised action. I hung the phone up and swayed as I yawned. One tired dungbeetle. I decided to take the rest of the day off. The Copra would need checking and anyway my head ached. I headed for bed.

Six hours later I was one happy dungbeetle. Stripping down a fast dung-roll is an absorbing job, only surpassed by putting it together again. I was a lucky dungbeetle too. The bluebottle patrol had hit the place just in time: a team of maggots was about to begin breaking her up. They'd been taken in for questioning. As I stepped out of the elevator I heard the phone ringing in my apartment.

It was Buzz – and his news took the smile clean from my face. I'd hoped that the maggots would sing. I wanted to know who was behind the attack.

'They died, Buzz? They all died? Every last maggot?'

I could almost hear Buzz swallow hard. 'That's right, Sir.' Buzz was a smart kid. He couldn't believe it either.

'What did they die of?'

This time I *did* hear Buzz swallow hard. He didn't want to tell me. 'Food poisoning.'

'Food poisoning?' I screamed. 'No maggot in the

world ever got food poisoning! There's no such thing as a maggot with bad digestion! Buzz, what the hell is going on down at that precinct of yours?'

Now the young cop was really nervous. 'I can't tell you, Mr Dungbeetle,' he whispered. 'Not over the phone. But something's wrong.' I was agreeing when Buzz suddenly said 'Thank you, ma'am. You call right back if your greenfly is still missing at dusk and we'll see what we can do.' The line went dead and I guessed that maybe the Chief had walked in on him. I was also thinking that maybe the Chief had walked in on the maggots too – and stopped them dead in their tracks.

I drove over to the office in late afternoon to check the mail. There was a message: *After the late show in my dressing-room*. It was signed L.

I stood at the bar and looked discreetly round. The Flea Pit was packed for the late show and Big Daddy and the Chief were at their table, waiting to hear Lady sing. The band finished a number and the dancers drifted back to their tables. The lights dimmed and in the dark I stepped through the door. I could hear Lady singing but she sounded far away. I found the door with the star and tapped gently. There was no answer. I went in.

Hands went round my neck and tightened. Automatically I ducked and swivelled, swinging my whole body into my assailant who lost his grip and hit the wall heavily. I pulled air through my bruised throat as I moved in on him. Then I stopped. 'Buzz?'

139

Buzz shook his head a few times and gazed up at me through a tornado of spinning stars. 'Mr Dungbeetle?' he gasped as I reached down to pull him to his feet.

We talked fast. I asked the rookie bluebottle what he was doing here and he told me there'd been a message for him at home. He told me how the Chief had taken the maggots down to the cells – after which they'd never been seen again.

'What you saying, Buzz?'

'I'm saying he must have killed them.'

I told him how I saw the deathwatch beetle with Big Daddy and the Chief. I told him I was investigating the dungbeetle disappearances and was building up a picture with Big Daddy square in the frame.

I swung the door open. Big Daddy was outside. Behind him was the Chief.

'Dungbeetle,' the Chief said in his clumsy way, 'didn't I always say you'd come to a sticky end?'

'Did you have to kill your prisoners?'

The Chief grinned. 'Come on, Dungbeetle. You gonna thump your thorax over a bunch of lousy maggots? What's your problem? You a secret maggot-lover or something?'

'Listen, Chief,' I said, more bravely than I felt, 'playing big with maggots is one thing. Mixing it with one of your own cops and a private investigator is another. You going to arrest *us*? Take us down to your cells? You can't. You've got nothing on us.'

The Chief whistled. To my horror I saw something

small walk down the wall right where we'd been talking. It was a bug. It walked over to the Chief. 'That's right,' he grinned. 'This room is bugged. It got every word you said.'

Distantly, through the open door, I heard Lady's song come to an end and applause drift through. Big Daddy spoke. 'Outside. Now.'

I shifted my balance ready to jump but the Chief smiled a deeply unpleasant smile. 'Don't even think about it, son,' he drawled. He stood aside and the biggest stag-beetle I ever saw squeezed through the door so its stink filled the room. Buzz groaned quietly. I groaned noisily. We both groaned again together.

Me and Buzz sat very still in Big Daddy's office. The stag was behind us and I knew he'd be looking at us hungrily. The bright light from the lamp was troubling to our eyes. We couldn't see through its dazzle to the Chief and Big Daddy. We listened to the bug.

I heard myself. 'What you saying, Buzz?'

I heard Buzz. 'I'm saying he must have killed them.'

There was silence. 'OK, Dungbeetle,' whispered Big Daddy. 'Who's your client? Who's paying you to ask dumb questions at City Hall?' He was at his most dangerous when he was quiet like this.

'Go take a running jump at yourself.' I figured our only chance was to make him lose his cool. 'Your legs are long enough.'

The Chief sniggered. Big Daddy spoke again, his

voice even quieter. 'Your dungbeetle sense of humour is going to get you killed.' The stag-beetle panted. I could feel its breath on my neck.

'You want me to talk?' I said. 'OK. Tell this overgrown and underbrained less-than-incredible hulk of yours to back off.' The stag snorted menacingly but Big Daddy must have signalled because I felt it take a step or so away.

The Chief spoke. 'Buzz,' he said casually, 'who's Dungbeetle's client and what's the interest in Department Z?'

Buzz said a brave thing – braver than all my wisecracks. 'My father was a good cop, Chief, and he always told me there is nothing lower than a bent bluebottle. I'm just glad he's not around to see this.' Buzz spat into the darkness behind the lamp.

I began to murmur, 'Take it easy, Buzz.'

Too late. I couldn't see the signal and the stag moved fast. I heard the unmistakable ripping of wings but before Buzz could cry out the stag tore off his head. It had been terrible but it had been quick. I felt that hot breath on my neck and, believe me, I said nothing and I did nothing as I tried to get my brain out of shock.

'So. Now will the dungbeetle talk?' Big Daddy's voice was deadly.

'He better,' said the Chief and chuckled just as the door opened and Lady walked in. I only knew it was her because of the couple of words she said before she screamed, seeing me drenched in Buzz's blood.

I took the chance and jumped for the lamp as the antlers slashed at me. In the dark I made for the door. I reached for Lady but she wasn't there. I could hear her scuffling with Big Daddy and the Chief so I knew she was alive. The stag came crashing after me as I hit the air, and I made the quiet sidestreet where I'd parked the Copra just outside the Olympic record for five hundred centimetres. Thirty seconds later I was heading out of town fast. The streetlights dropped behind and I pushed up the speed. I tried to put Buzz out of my mind. There'd be a time for remembering him but it wasn't yet. I tried to put Lady out of my mind too but that wasn't easy either.

The hermit termites were chanting dawn prayers as I followed white-robed Brother Adam through the galleries of the colony. I was glad to have him show me the way. Every time I came to the valley to visit Odonata it seemed to me I was taken by a different path. I was beginning to ask myself if it had a meaning. That's how it is with religious insects – they never come out with anything straight. They leave it for you to work out yourself.

The Master was hovering over his stream, meditating. Brother Adam left and I made a rough try at the only yoga position I could hold for ten minutes without falling over. Like always, the troubles of the metropolis seemed far away. I think I slept but I'm not sure. Next thing I knew was Odonata quiet at my side. Odonata.

The wisest creature I ever knew. In my book that made him the toughest.

'So the dungbeetle comes to the dragonfly?'

'How ya doing, Master?'

We didn't speak for a bit. There wasn't any need. But suddenly I was thinking of Lady and Buzz and he saw my sadness.

'Tell me.'

I told him. I sensed his mind moving over the information, picking up the bits that made no sense and fitting them back in the story. Finally he told me what I needed to know. I was shocked. I was scared. I had to leave fast. He understood.

'One day you will stay here a long time, Derek. Maybe the rest of your life.'

Then his wings flicked and I watched him shimmer back over the water. I realised Brother Adam was waiting to lead me back to the Copra and real life – or maybe the real life was right there by the stream. I don't know. That's how the valley gets me.

I didn't drive back to the metropolis. The Copra seemed hardly to touch the ground as I headed through the desert. One dungbeetle in a hurry.

I should have made one of the connections myself. Once a week a shipment left the metropolis and headed along the dung-trail to the next state. They were in a bad way there. Nothing would grow. There were insects starving and selling them high-grade muck was a major source of the metropolis' income. We had plenty to spare. The city founders were smart. They'd settled near the cow plains. This inter-state trade had been in place two years now and the shipments were under the control of the dungbeetles. Who else? I came to the bottom of the ridge and changed gear as I powered up.

I hadn't seen a shipment on the move for a while and it was some sight. I guess I was looking down on five hundred dungbeetles, each with a load two or three times its height, moving at the same pace with the regulation gap between them. It was a fine sight. I could have stood and cheered.

Then, out of nowhere, a hover-fly swooped low over the shipment and I changed my mind. I kept very still and checked the Copra was hidden. I guessed the hover-fly was sending a message and wondered who to. I shouldn't have asked. Twelve black thorns rose above a low hill directly ahead of the dung trail. The twelve thorns grew to twelve menacing antlers. The twelve antlers were fixed on six stag-beetles. The shipment braked. I waited for the massacre.

No massacre. I tried to make sense of what was happening. Then from behind the same hill – was the sun playing tricks? – I saw another line of dungbeetles appear further along the trail. I focused my binoculars. They were tired, ragged, underfed, and their loads looked pale and dry. I was watching a hijack. And a substitution. The hover-fly was circling again. At its signal the new five hundred set off wearily towards the border with two stag-beetles guarding them while the others forced the genuine shipment off the dung-trail into the scrub. One smooth operation and the next moment there was nothing. I might have dreamed it. No chance.

The entrance to the tunnel was hidden in desert scrub and there were no guards. Whoever was running this operation was either stupid or very confident.

The tunnel was wide. I moved fast and kept my eyes open the best I could in the dark but there was nobody around. The floor was caked in high-grade dung but the rich aromatic odour was ruined by the rank smell of stag. Way ahead I saw the suggestion of light and five minutes later I came out of the tunnel and looked down. Suddenly I knew where the missing dungbeetles and glow-worms had gone.

A cavern had been carved out of the desert rock, eight galleries deep. It reminded me of the termite colony – only THIS WAS BIG and everywhere there were dungbeetles working. Way down at the bottom the stolen shipment was being broken up and stored away. Hundreds of glow-worms were lighting the fantastic operation. I looked for a door big enough for the stags to get through and found it on the lowest level. If they needed reinforcements that's the way they were going to come.

So this was what it was about. The weekly shipments

of top-class dung were being hijacked and replaced by cheap low-grade muck. Somebody was building up an unsuspected fortune under the desert where only the dung-trains came. Whoever built this complex, planned this operation and was covering up the disappearances had to be an evil genius and I only knew one. I had to get back to the metropolis and talk to a few councillors. I hoped they'd believe me. I turned to the tunnel. That was when I heard Lady sing.

> 'So please someone come and help me.
> I don' know what to do.'

I froze. She was alive. She was here. I tried to get her direction but the cavern was full of echoes. Others heard her too. Dungbeetles were looking round and murmuring to each other. One of them shouted something. But then Big Daddy was out on Level Five and the Chief was hammering on one of the doors with his riot stick and Lady's voice cut out. The Chief yelled down to the stags who moved menacingly in on the slaves – and they got right back to work. Fast. Nobody noticed one more dungbeetle moving down to Level Five.

I listened at the door. I tried the handle. Lady's voice was sharp, scared. 'Who's there?'

'Hey listen, Lady,' I said. 'I don't give up on a client till she's paid her bill, OK?'

I heard her gasp and soon she was right the other side of the door as I turned my personal all-purpose key in the lock. We began the climb to the level above. 'This is worrying,' I said. 'It shouldn't be as easy as this.' And suddenly it wasn't.

I don't know who saw us but a siren began to wail. Up above, a slab of rock slid down to shut off the tunnel and, down below, stags were pushing through their big door. Easy? I should have kept my big mouth shut.

We made Level Six and I almost had my foot on the ladder to Level Seven when it was winched up. We were marooned. Now the stags were on Three, moving up, and Big Daddy and the Chief were with them. All stags look alike to me but I recognised Bonzo from the Flea Pit and sure as hell it recognised me. As it reached Level Six it sighed happily and dribbled.

I looked down at the dungbeetles crowding the bottom of the cavern. I had to spur them to action. The echoes carried my voice to every level.

'You call yourselves dungbeetles? Nobody in a million years could imagine that anybody – *anybody* – could make slaves of a thousand dungbeetles!'

I had their attention but did I have time? I glanced towards Bonzo who was waiting for Big Daddy to give the signal. Big Daddy had a mocking smile on his face. The Chief sniggered. I licked my lips and glanced at Lady. She nodded encouragingly.

'A thousand dungbeetles enslaved by a handful of second-rate stags with brains so small you'd lose them in a sand pit? OK now you've got the chance to do something about it!' They were all watching and listening now. 'Creation has entrusted dungbeetles with a sacred task! The dung must get through! The show must go on! What are we? Dorks or dungbeetles?'

The silence was intense. Big Daddy clapped mockingly. 'Nice try, Dungbeetle.' He gestured to the stag. It flexed its antlers which cracked like a gunshot and I saw every dungbeetle in that cavern cringe. Some looked away – they didn't want to see what was going to happen. I didn't want to see it either. Bonzo scratched in the dust at his feet like stags always do before they rush. I kept my eyes on the stag but my words were meant for Big Daddy.

'OK, bigshot, I just hope you can live with yourself for what you're doing over the border. Larvae are crying for food over there – dying from hunger – while you're stockpiling the best organic muck in the world out of greed. The pale stuff you're sending them wouldn't grow watercress. That make you proud?'

Big Daddy smiled. 'It's going to make me rich, Dungbeetle. There's a world-wide shortage coming. That means food won't get grown; folks will go hungry. Best of all, it means fear. And fear is my trade. When the riots are over and civilisation's on its knees,' smiled Big Daddy, 'the world will come begging to me for muck. Muck is power, Dungbeetle, and it's going to make me the most powerful insect in the world.'

I tried to laugh and it came out OK. 'Well well well,' I cackled, 'so it's just the crazy-ruler-of-the-world show after all! Grow up, longlegs. Get a life!'

Big Daddy didn't like it. He waved Bonzo forward

and the antlers clashed a millimetre from my throat. Lady screamed. I pushed her behind me – not that I was going to be great protection for long. Then the stag swung its bulk sideways at me and all my legs left the ground. I hit the rock behind me and slid into a heap as the stag-antler whipped my face – left side, right side, left side, right side. I could hear Lady begging Big Daddy to stop it. Then another voice echoed round the cavern and into my aching head.

'He's right! Are we dungbeetles or not? Are we going to let this happen?'

A young dungbeetle was shouting from Level One and Lady was staring down at him with shining eyes. 'Donald . . .' she murmured.

'They kill us. They starve us. They punish us. Let's get mad. Let's get even! Hell hath no fury like a dungbeetle scorned! What are we waiting for? Let's kick thorax!'

A roar rose from the floor of the cavern as the dungbeetles attacked. Big Daddy and the Chief peered down unbelievingly. As Bonzo leaned over the edge – to see his fellow bonzos staggering under the weight of a thousand biting, gouging, kicking, punching dung-beetles – I made the only move I could. I dodged behind the Chief and, using all my rolling skills and the last of my strength, I bounced him against the stag. They tottered on the edge. The bellowing stag was desperate for something to hang on to and the only thing in reach was the Chief. The razor-sharp antlers sliced him in half as neatly as they'd dispatched Buzz to the great cowpat in the sky, while down on the lowest level the last stag was feebly kicking inside its coating of dungbeetles and the others lay around like wrecked tanks after a battle.

Lady was already hurrying down to Donald who was hurrying up toot damn sweet as Big Daddy watched his dreams bite the dust. I quietly reached in through one of the doors and found a large ball of soft dung. Big Daddy turned towards me, his face distorted in fury. 'I'll get you for this, Dungbeetle,' he snarled.

'On your own head be it,' I replied, jamming it over his shoulders with much pleasure, might and malice.

'Mmmhgnnh!' Big Daddy insisted.

'Certainly,' I replied, spinning to dish out a Derek Dungbeetle speciality – a rapid tattoo of karate kicks with each of my six legs. I did it twice. And once again for luck (mine, not Big Daddy's).

The worms glowed and the music played as Lady walked into the spotlight. The Flea Pit was packed and applause rocked the joint. I took a swig of liquor and looked to where the table near the office used to be. Not any more. Big Daddy was in the metropolis penitentiary waiting for a different kind of show – his trial. There was silence as Lady sang the blues and it seemed to me her voice had an extra quality tonight.

'Well I woke up this mornin' – things were looking blue.
Oh yes I woke up this mornin' and things were really blue.
When my lover went away he took my heart along too.'

Lady knew where I was sitting. She sang especially for me.

> 'I had the ladybird blues –
> Oh yes, those ladybird blues.
> Couldn't fight.
>
> 'I had the ladybird blues –
> Was gonna blow my fuse.
> I was so uptight.'

She reached down to a table as close to the stage as it could get, where Donald was smiling up. The spotlight held them both. He stood. They kissed.

> 'But now my lover's with me – and everything's all right.'

Yeah. Everything was all right. Lady had her guy; Donald had his dame. Every two days over the next month a shipment of Big Daddy's stockpile was going to make life a whole lot better for our neighbours across the border. I grinned and clapped with the rest. Then I went out into the metropolis night. I drove the Copra through the empty streets with thoughts of bed and smiled. Tomorrow I had unfinished business with the tick-head from Department Z. Around the Oak-Elm intersection it began to rain and I smiled some more because that's the sort of weather a weary dungbeetle likes. Be lucky, OK?

EVERYTHING MUST GO
Ian Strachan

Illustrated by Jonathan Heale

I've been sitting in the drizzle, on the top of the hill above our farm all day, watching the crowds following the auctioneer round the outbuildings while he sells the various lots.

There's no way I could have stayed down there. It'd be like watching thieves looting the place, or vultures picking meat off the bones of a dead animal.

It was bad enough when Grandad made me help the auctioneer's men get it all ready. Stuff came out of the buildings which I'd never even seen before.

'Oh, that's a cheesepress,' Grandad explained proudly, when they dragged out a great cobwebbed lump of machinery. 'We used to make all our own. I remember the time . . .'

But the men were too busy sticking big, black numbers on everything, for the auction catalogue, to listen to any of Grandad's stories.

One of the things we unearthed looked as if a set of bagpipes had been grafted onto a violin! Grandad explained it was a seed-fiddle, which he last used when he was a lad to hand-sew the ten-acre field with grass seed.

'Who on earth will buy a thing like that?' I asked.

'The same kind of half-baked idiot as bought my old horse plough, covered it with gloss paint and bolted it to the wall of his house!'

The one thing I really didn't want to see go was my tractor. I loved driving it and I spent hours ploughing and everything. It was like a second home to me and I was never happier than when I was out on it.

My grandad's down there now, but he's stayed in the house and says he won't come out until everyone's cleared off. A few of his old cronies turned up early and they've sat in the back kitchen drinking beer with him, just like they did after Grandma's funeral.

I've been dreading this day for weeks, ever since Grandad dropped the bombshell about having to sell up the farm.

'It's no good, Neil, I just can't make a living no more,' he said. 'I'm only what they call a dog-and-stick farmer. There's no room nowadays for people with only a few acres. Some of these great big farms get more each year in grants for growin' nowt than I can earn through hard work.'

'But what'll happen to this place?'

'These days there's no choice,' Grandad said bitterly. 'It'll simply be swallowed up by one of the farms around us. They'll keep most of the land and sell the house with a few acres to one of the horse Mafia.'

Grandad has always hated the rich townies who've come out and bought up most of the old cottages and small farms, at prices the locals can't possibly afford. 'All that so their kids can try and ride their fat ponies for a couple of hours at weekends!'

I still couldn't believe he was really going to sell up. 'But you always said Dad could have this place when you retired.'

'So did I, lad,' Grandad said wistfully. 'So did I.'

From the time he left school, until five years ago, Dad had worked alongside Grandad, but then came the first sign that things were going badly. There was so little money coming in, Dad had been forced to take a job in a factory miles from the village.

I was staggered by the change which came over my dad. Almost overnight he lost his rugged, weather-tanned look and became all grey and pinched. Mind you, Dad reckoned, at his age, he was lucky to get a job at all. But he stopped coming home full of stories about what he'd been doing, as he had when he worked on the farm. He just read the paper, or fell asleep in front of the telly.

Even so, I'd still managed to kid myself that it was going to be all right for me when I left school next year. I was convinced I'd still go and work full-time for Grandad, instead of just the evenings, school holidays and weekends I'd been doing.

With the farm gone, I haven't a clue what's going to happen to me. I've spent every single hour at school just daydreaming about escaping. Even if there were any jobs at the factory, and lately they've been laying people off, I don't want to be stuck indoors. Even when the weather's cold and wet, I'd sooner be in the open air, where you can hear birds sing and watch foxes stalking their prey. I don't mind listening to pop music while I'm driving the tractor round but that's not the same as having it booming out of the factory loudspeaker week in, week out.

It's been a slow death for the old place. First the property was sold, next the stock went and finally there's this sale of all the machinery and stuff.

I knew Grandad was really going to sell up when flocks of people came rubbernecking round the farm the minute the property was advertised. Half of them weren't really interested, just nosy. But even the ones who were, could be so downright rude. They came at all hours of the day and night, often without an appointment or bothering to announce themselves. I was collecting eggs once and found two complete strangers *inside* our hen-house.

Worst of all were the smart remarks some of them made in front of Grandad. 'Of course the house isn't worth keeping. We'd have to get a bulldozer in and clear the site completely.' The way they talked, you'd never have thought they were in someone's home.

Many's the time I've nearly been knocked off my bike into the ditch as they come roaring round our narrow lanes in their shiny, Japanese, four-wheel-drive jeeps. The only off-road driving most of them have ever done is when they park on the pavements in town. They complain about the mud and at night wonder, 'How do you manage without streetlights?'

If they stopped in the village and asked, in their snooty voices, for directions to Grandad's farm, the locals took great delight in sending them round the longest way they could think of!

They thought nothing of parking in gateways, blocking everyone's way. Which was why I wasn't a bit surprised, one Saturday afternoon, to find another one stuck across a field gate. But the main difference with this one, apart from the fact it was pointing towards the village and not the farm, was that it was jacked up, with a rear wheel off.

A ginger-bearded bloke flagged me down. 'Sorry to bother you but I've got a bit of a problem.'

'Yes, I can see that.'

'The *real* problem is,' he said, with an embarrassed grin, 'my spare's flat too. I noticed a garage in the village and I wondered if they could help?'

I shook my head. 'They're only open for petrol Saturday afternoons. The mechanic, Dave, is off by now.'

'What's the problem, Dad?'

The passenger door opened and this girl, about my age, wearing black jeans and a sloppy green sweater, climbed out. You may think it stupid, but the first thing that struck me about her was, her sensible wellington boots were neither green, nor particularly clean. You'd be amazed how many high-heeled women brought their children to look at the farm wearing sandals and were surprised when their white socks turned a soggy khaki in the mucky puddles.

Her father told her, 'The mechanic at the garage has finished for the day, Sally.'

Sally sighed, but spoke to me as if she could tell I'd understand how much we trusted grown-ups. 'Mum told him to get the spare fixed days ago.'

'Bad luck really,' I said sympathetically. 'They were hedge-cutting round here this week and there's always thorns about.'

'I suppose,' the man said, 'I'll have to find a phone and ring the AA, but they could take a while to get out here.'

Sally wasn't willing to give up so easily. 'Do you know,' she asked me, 'where the mechanic lives?'

'Dave lives out on the main road.'

'Well, maybe,' she suggested, 'you could ride round and ask him if he'd be willing to help us?'

'That's asking a lot,' her father said.

'You'll just have to pay him extra,' Sally insisted. 'After all, it is your own fault.'

Her father smiled. 'That's not what I was talking about. I meant, why should our friend here want to waste his Saturday afternoon, just because I haven't got the sense to remember to get the spare wheel fixed?'

'Oh, I don't mind,' I said quickly.

And that's what happened. Dave came out with his truck and Sally thought I was a knight in shining armour, especially when I not only returned with Dave, but with three cans of Coke too.

'Oh, thanks,' she said, 'you're a *real* life-saver!'

That was when I first noticed the openness of Sally's smile. She had blue eyes, short dark hair and pale skin, but with bright red cheeks and lips which really parted when she smiled.

'I'm Neil, by the way,' I said, opening a can and passing it to her. She had nice hands with sensible nails. The girls at school have competitions to see how long they can grow them and then have fits when one breaks. I'm not much into girls. Most of the ones at school are really stupid. I've only got to mention shooting rabbits for them to go all stupid and they think it's really smart to pretend I smell of cow muck.

But Sally was different. She didn't mess about, acting all shy, and her dad wasn't bad either, for a townie with a beard! 'You obviously live round here, Neil,' he said, while Dave had gone to the garage to mend the punctures.

'Yes, I live in the council houses.'

'It seems good land round here.'

'Some is,' I said, 'but Grandad reckons a lot of it's dying from the amount of weedkiller and artificial fertiliser that's been dumped on it. He says it's more like a science lab than fields and all the life's gone out of it.'

'Yes, that's the trouble these days,' the man agreed.

'My grandad says there's nothing to beat lots of cow manure and resting fields between crops. That's what he does.'

'Oh, your grandfather's a farmer, is he?'

'He is at the moment, over at Leasow Farm,' I said, 'but he's got to sell up. Can't make ends meet. We've worked hard to make a go of it, but you can't compete with the big boys these days.'

'You help him, do you, Neil?'

'Always have, ever since I was little.' Not wanting to sound like a kid playing at it, I quickly added, 'I do most of the tractor work now Grandad's getting on a bit.'

'Really?'

'Yes,' I said, without a word of a lie, 'I did all the ploughing and haymaking this year.'

'That's a very responsible job,' the man said, stroking his beard. 'I suppose you'll be looking for farm work when you leave school? When is that?'

'Next year, when I'm sixteen. But there's not much work on farms round here. They just get contractors in when they need them, rather than employ farm-workers of their own.'

That was when Dave came back with the wheels and the man went off to lend a hand.

We hardly had time to say goodbye before they were off, heading towards town. They obviously weren't going to look at the farm at all.

But just before their car went round the bend, I could have sworn Sally turned to look back at me. Dave must have noticed too, judging by the way he nudged me in the ribs and said, 'I think you made a bit of a hit there, Neil!'

'Give over,' I said, picking up my bike. 'What would I want with a bunch of townies?'

'Ah, well, suit yourself,' Dave said, 'but meeting them didn't do me any harm.' He brandished the two twenty-pound notes he'd been paid for helping them.

'That's the trouble with townies, Grandad says. They've got more money than sense,' I said bitterly.

'I can understand how your grandad feels,' Dave said, 'but my livelihood depends on the incomers. I couldn't make a living just out of the locals.'

'But I thought they all took their posh cars to work with them and have them serviced in town.'

Dave nodded. 'That they do. But I still get to work on all the second and third cars they own and without them I'd have had to shut down long ago. Then the locals wouldn't have a garage any more and they'd have to drive ten miles just to buy petrol. Times are changing,' Dave said, as he hauled himself up into his truck, 'and you just have to make the best of it if you want to survive.'

When the farm itself sold for an astronomical price, Grandad wasn't the least bit pleased. 'If I'd had that sort of money when I still *had* the farm,' he grumbled, 'I could have stayed in business, updated the machinery and bought new blood into the stock. As it is,' he sighed, 'apart from buying a few drinks down at the Fox it isn't going to be a lot of use at my time of life.'

'But who bought it?' I asked.

'I don't rightly know,' the old man said. 'I left the moment the hammer went down, but Harry said it was an organist. Another of these arty-farty types.'

A few weeks later the stock went, even the hens. In all honesty, the herd wasn't worth much in terms of money, but the line went back to my great-grandfather and Grandad had hand-reared some of them as calves. They meant a lot to him and he was really down the day they were carted off.

The farm sale of all the equipment, including the old tractor I'd always thought of as mine, was like knocking the last nail in the coffin.

Grandad had read the notice of the sale they'd pasted up on the gatepost. There was a short list of items on offer. The old man shook his head. 'Not much to show for a life, is it? I'm only glad your grandmother didn't live long enough to see everyone picking over our bits and pieces.' Then his eye caught the poster's last line, printed in heavy black type: *Everything Must Go*. 'Isn't that the truth?' he said bitterly. 'And me with it!'

As I started to walk down the hill towards the farm, the last cars were pulling out of the yard with their booty. The cheesepress was lashed on somebody's roof rack. Scrappy Clarke's battered pick-up truck was piled high with rolls of wire netting and sheets of rusty galvanised iron.

A watery sun was sinking slowly over the hill and its misty rays made the damp cobblestones glisten as if they were on fire.

About this time, any other day, we would have been finishing milking. The yard would have been alive with the sounds of the generator, the soft clunk of buckets and the click of cattle hooves on straw, as they shifted in their stalls. I'd hear Grandad's raised voice, as he slapped a cow's rump, to make it shift over, then the clink of chains and the hiss of the milking-cups as they went on the next teats. Above it all, would have been the middle of the road music of Radio 2, which Grandad always reckoned made them milk easier.

But not today.

It was like walking through a ghost town. Grandad was right about the place dying.

Out of habit I shut the byre door, which was swinging loosely in the wind, and then realised there was no point. The only thing that might escape were the rats, now their food supply was gone.

When I saw the farmhouse all in darkness, I thought at first Grandad must have gone off to the Fox with some of his mates. I opened the back door and the scrape of my heels on the tiled floor echoed round the empty kitchen.

Grandad made me jump when he asked, 'Is that you, Neil?'

Though his voice came from the direction of his usual place, tonight the fire had died to little more than a dull glow, his chair had been sold with the rest and he was standing, gazing out of the window.

'Why are you sitting alone in the dark like this, Grandad? Shall I put the light on?'

'No, lad, leave it. I just wanted to stay quiet a minute or two before we walk up to your place,' he said. Grandad had already moved his belongings up to our house, but he'd been spending every day at the farm, just as if he still had work to do.

'It's all over, lad,' he said quietly, 'and nowt to show for it!'

'You've got a lot of money though, Grandad,' I gently pointed out.

'Oh, money, aye! I suppose I could always go on a world cruise. God knows, I won't have much else to do with my time.'

'But some of that money helped get Dad out of the factory,' I pointed out. Grandad had bought Dad some petrol-driven equipment, including a mower, a strimmer and hedge-cutter, so that he could do garden-maintenance work. It seems a lot of the people who've bought these big places are too busy earning the money to pay for them to look after their own gardens. 'So at least it's done Dad a bit of good.'

'I suppose,' Grandad said glumly. 'Come on, let's get out of here.'

Slowly, for the very last time, he locked the back door and just stopped himself from, out of habit, slipping it under the stone, where he'd kept it. Instead he dropped it into the pocket of his overalls and we were setting off across the yard, when I heard a noise.

'Grandad,' I said, 'there's somebody in our orchard.'

Three figures were slipping between the trees in the twilight.

'It isn't *our* orchard any more,' Grandad growled. 'It's theirs – they're the new owners. Maybe you should meet them.'

'No, thanks,' I said firmly. 'Let's go.'

But before I'd moved a step, a girl's voice cut through the darkness. 'Hi, Neil, wait a minute.'

I turned and saw Sally stepping out of the shadows. She was followed by her father and a woman in a headscarf, who I could easily see from her ready smile, was Sally's mother.

'I thought for a minute,' Sally said, 'you were going to run off without speaking.'

I could hardly get over my astonishment. 'I just didn't realise it was you who'd bought the place,' I burbled. I was delighted to see her again, though I knew it wouldn't affect the fate of the place. 'You'll have somewhere to keep your pony now.'

Sally looked puzzled. 'What on earth makes you think I'd even want a pony? Dad wanted the place.'

'But I thought he was a musician,' I said, thinking it would explain the beard.

But Sally looked even more confused. 'What are you talking about?'

'Grandad told me the place had been bought by an organist!'

Sally laughed. 'Dad may be going to pull out all the stops, but he's tone-deaf and into organ*ics*, organic growing.'

'Which was why,' Sally's father said, coming up and slipping an arm round his daughter's shoulder, 'although I'd already seen the farm when you rescued us, I was so interested to get your honest information about the land.' He turned to his wife. 'This is Neil, the boy I told you about.'

'Hello, Neil,' she said with a cheerful grin. 'I think I'd have recognised you from Sally's description.'

'Mum!' Sally murmured and I was pleased to see she blushed slightly.

'Thing is,' the man went on, as if he hadn't heard a word anyone else had said, 'I want to make a go of this place.'

'I tried that and look where it got me!' Grandad said. I'd almost forgotten he was still there.

'My idea's rather different,' the man said gently. 'I specialise in herbs.'

Grandad's mouth dropped open. 'You mean you've

bought my place to grow sage and parsley? Now, I think I've heard everything!'

'Not exactly. They're rather more unusual herbs and I wouldn't grow them for the kitchen, but for the pharmaceutical industry. They guarantee to buy my entire crop, but the soil they're grown on has to be pure, untainted by any chemicals. But the point is, to get this project off the ground,' the man said, 'I'm going to need some help. I'll have to keep my present job at least for the first year, until this business gets established. Neil, you've worked the land for your grandfather – would you do the same for me? I mean, by the time you leave school, the whole project should be up and running and I might be able to offer you a full-time job.'

I could see Sally, who was standing just behind her father, nodding eagerly, but I didn't need any encouragement. 'Yes, of course, I'd love to. It's only a shame my old tractor was sold off today.'

It was her father's turn to smile. 'Yes, well, I took a chance you'd agree to stay on and I bought it.'

'That's fantastic! Did you hear that, Grandad? It's all going to be . . .'

But when I turned round, Grandad was halfway across the yard, on his way to our house. He knew the good news wasn't for him, his time was over.

'Neil,' Sally said, 'while Mum and Dad do some measuring up in the house, could we take your tractor on a celebration run round some of the fields?'

Her father looked totally bewildered. 'But it's pitch-dark, you won't be able to see a thing.'

But his wife laughed. 'Don't be silly, dear!' she said, leading him towards the house.

Sally looked me straight in the eye and said, 'Ready to give my my first driving lesson?'

I couldn't help smiling. 'Aye, come on.'

But, as we turned into the field, the beam from the tractor headlights flashed over the hunched figure of Grandad, plodding towards our house, where he'd end his days, only able to look at the land to which he'd devoted his entire life.

But at least Grandad would have the satisfaction of knowing his work hadn't gone for nothing. No diggers would be coming along to rip out all the hedges and turn it into one big field and Sally's dad obviously wouldn't be killing the ground off with bag fertilisers and pesticides. Even if it wasn't in our family any longer, the farm would go on being a living thing.

ABOUT THE AUTHORS

Rachel Anderson has won the Guardian Children's Fiction Award and the Medical Journalists Award. She lives in North Norfolk and likes growing strawberries. Amongst her titles for children are *Princess Jazz and the Angels* and *Letters from Heaven*.

Berlie Doherty is an acclaimed writer for adults and children. Her books in Mammoth include *How Green You Are!*, *Children of Winter*, *White Peak Farm* and *Tilly Mint Tales*. She has won the Carnegie Medal twice, for *Granny Was a Buffer Girl*, and *Dear Nobody*.

Anthony Horowitz is a prolific writer for television. His work includes *Poirot*, *Heroes & Villains*, *Chiller* and *Murder Most Horrid*. He has won several prizes in England and Europe for his children's books . . . most recently for *South by South East*, chosen as 1995 Book of the Year in France. His other titles include *Granny* (soon to be filmed), *Groosham Grange* and *The Falcon's Malteser*.

Ted Hughes, President of Farms for City Children, was appointed Poet Laureate in 1984. Much of his verse has been written for children, such as *What is the Truth?* which won the Guardian Fiction award in 1985, and *The Cat and the Cuckoo*, dedicated to the children who come to the Farms for City Children. He has also written many modern children's classics: *The Iron Man*, *Meet My Folks*, *Nessie, the Mannerless Monster*, and most recently, *The Iron Woman*, the sequel to *The Iron Man*.

He was born in Yorkshire and now lives in the West Country.

Dick King-Smith has written many popular books for children, mostly about animals. These include *The Mouse Butcher*, *Saddlebottom* and *The Sheep-pig*, which won the 1984 Guardian

Children's Fiction Award. He has also written *Friends and Brothers* and *Lightning Strikes Twice*, both available in Mammoth, and *Lightning Fred*, a Banana book.

Elizabeth Laird is an award-winning writer whose most recent novel, *Hiding Out* won the Smarties Young Judges Award. *Kiss the Dust* was chosen as Children's Book of the Year by the Federation of Children's Book Groups. Her other titles include *Red Sky in the Morning, Crackers* and *Pink Ghost of Lamont*.

Joanna Lumley was born in Kashmir in 1946. She was educated in England at an Anglican convent; after three years as a photographic model she obtained an equity card and started a career as an actress. She has appeared in many films, television shows and stage plays. Her recent successes include her BAFTA award-winning performance in *Absolutely Fabulous*. Joanna is the author of several books. She has one son, Jamie, and is married to the conductor Stephen Barlow. They live in London.

Bel Mooney has a high profile as an adult author, broadcaster and journalist as well as being an environmental campaigner and an extraordinarily successful children's author. Her books include *The Voices of Silence* as well as the popular Kitty series: *Why not?, But you promised!, I know!, It's not fair!, I can't find it!, I don't want to!, I'm scared!* and *I wish!* She has also written *The Mouse with Many Rooms* for younger children.

Michael Morpurgo has been a teacher and a farmer. As a writer he has produced outstanding and best-selling fiction for children and young adults. He lives on a farm in Devon with his wife, Clare, and together they run Farms for City Children, the charity that they founded more than twenty years ago. Michael's many titles include *The Wreck of the Zanzibar, The War of Jenkins' Ear, Waiting for Anya* and *Why the Whales Came*, and amongst his Banana books are *Colly's Barn, Jo-Jo the Melon Donkey* and *The Marble Crusher*.

Alick Rowe has been a teacher and is an award-winning radio

171

and television dramatist. His first novel for children, *Voices of Danger*, was commended for the Carnegie Medal. He has written a second novel, *The Panic Wall*.

Ian Strachan writes brilliantly about children up against the odds, as he did in *The Boy in the Bubble*, winner of the Federation of Children's Book Groups Award and The Lancashire Book Award. *The Flawed Glass* was shortlisted for the Whitbread Award and *throwaways* for the Sheffield Book Award. Ian has written two books about the Vietnam boat children, *Journey of a Thousand Miles* and *The Second Step* and his titles include *Pebble on the Beach, Kidnap!*, and for younger readers, *The Upside Down World of Ginger Nutt* and *Wayne Loves Custard*.

FARMS FOR CITY CHILDREN

Charity Registration No. 325120R

Farms for City Children was established in 1976 as an educational charity to enrich the lives of city children. They come 35 at a time to live and work at three farms, Wick Court in Gloucestershire, Treginnis lsaf in Pembrokeshire and Nethercott House in Devon.

Of Wick Court Ted Hughes, the poet laureate, wrote:

'Old Wick with its five wizard hats
Wished in ghosts and prayed in bats
Till out of the dried up well of thirst
A fountain of new children burst
Then all Wick's memories trooped from sleep
Goats, ducks, chickens, cows, pigs, sheep.'

Of Treginnis Isaf he wrote:

'The animals and children of Treginnis
Hushed by the sea and the sky
Can hear a high gull cry
God rides in the wind above Treginnis.'

Of Nethercott House, the pioneer farm, the late Séan Rafferty, poet and gardener, wrote:

'Children come to the farms in Winter and Summer, in all seasons, in all weathers. Calves are born, foxes kill the chickens, sheep are dipped and shorn; and all this is not something which they watch – they are involved. THEY feed the hens, hiss at the geese, walk back from the milking parlour in the evening up a dark lane without street lamps, hear owls hoot in the night and are afraid.

Now more than ever it matters that children from the inner-cities can experience life in the country. This generation, which will hear repeatedly of ecological disaster, will be told that the earth itself is threatened. For some the earth will not be a globe in the classroom or a map on the wall but a Devon farm where they scuffled beech leaves along the drive and broke the ice on the puddles in the lane. When they are told of polluted rivers it will be one river, which has had its share of pollution, where they first saw a trout jumping and a wading heron, and plastic bags caught in the branches to mark the level of the last great flood. Last Spring two children went down to the river at dusk to watch for badgers. They did see a badger and they also saw two young otters at play, something many people born and bred in the country have never seen. It was as though Nature herself was choosing her champions.'

Séan Rafferty